Only the Fastest

The old man and his lovely niece Hope were in big trouble. The local land baron, bully-boy Aldo Latimer, wanted their ranch – at any cost.

But what made the old Clayton place worth so much to him? Why was he willing to try every dirty trick in the book to get it?

All Dick and Hope Clayton knew was that they needed protection … and when Buck Halliday rode in, they figured they'd found it.

Halliday wasn't looking for gun-work right then, but he liked the old man, and there was something about Hope that got under his skin and made him think it was time to settle down. So he signed on.

But the stakes were so high that soon, Halliday wasn't sure who he could really trust – not old Dick, not Hope … and certainly not his arch rival, Aldo Latimer's hired gun, Rees Mann.

Only the Fastest

Adam Brady

A Black Horse Western

ROBERT HALE

First published by Cleveland Publishing Co. Pty Ltd,
New South Wales, Australia
First published in 1967
© 2020 Mike Stotter and David Whitehead

This edition © The Crowood Press, 2020

ISBN 978-0-7198-3129-4

The Crowood Press
The Stable Block
Crowood Lane
Ramsbury
Marlborough
Wiltshire SN8 2HR

www.bhwesterns.com

Robert Hale is an imprint
of The Crowood Press

Typeset by
Simon and Sons ITES Services Pvt Ltd
Printed and bound in Great Britain by
4Bind Ltd, Stevenage, SG1 2XT

ONE

ALL TRAILS CLOSED

Sheriff Ted Lomar sat up with a start as shattering glass and snapping timber interrupted his afternoon nap. Jerking his head back, he lost his battered hat, and when grabbing it off the floor, skinned the tips of his fingers. Giving a deep-throated grunt, he took three strides into the street, stopped to plant the hat back on his head, then hitched up his pants and walked on.

In the late afternoon of a day hotter than any other that summer, Cannon Creek should have been quiet. It was not. In fact, Lomar, who liked to exert himself only as much as duty demanded, couldn't remember it ever being rowdier. He increased his pace at the sound of more breaking glass.

The community he protected lived in a typical frontier cow town. Long hitch racks lined the dusty streets at which horses drowsed while their owners sought mainly food, drink and the company of saloon girls. Most of the buildings had false fronts and just about all were weather-beaten and short of paint. Two saloons stood on opposite sides of the main street, each presenting a garishly painted front to the other. The dirt in the street between them was packed hard by the continual movement of wagons and human traffic. Much of the traveling was done by hard-drinking men seeking sanctuary in one saloon after being thrown out of the other.

Lomar knew all this, because it had been his misfortune, as he continually put it, to pin on a sheriff's badge four years ago. Since then he hadn't been able to find the energy to make a change for the better.

He stopped between the two saloons and eyed each establishment speculatively, before he turned toward the Lovely Lucy. It seemed to him that more noise was coming out of that place than from the Red Garter, but it was really the presence of Duke Timberlaine at the batwings of the Lovely Lucy that influenced him to check that watering hole out first.

He knew Timberlaine was a roughhouse fellow who had a talent for manhandling drunks. What else he could handle Lomar did not know, because Timberlaine was nowhere to be seen when the real hardcases got out of hand. He couldn't guess why Lucy Amour, as false a name as Lomar had ever heard, had hired the man. Perhaps Lucy, who'd been called Kate Smith by a drifter a year earlier, realized that what beauty she may have possessed had been lost in the bottoms of countless whiskey bottles. So why not take on Timberlaine if she could afford to have the handsome loafer about?

The lawman drew up on the porch, one hand planted on his gun butt, his stare fixed contemptuously on Timberlaine.

"What the hell's all that racket about?" Lomar demanded. Timberlaine adjusted a ruffle on his white silk shirt and frowned. "Racket, Sheriff? I don't hear none."

The front window of the saloon shattered under the hurtling body of a cowhand who landed a foot away from Timberlaine and went into a roll to finally hit his head against a rail. The cowboy made some incoherent noises, rose

7

to his feet, swayed, then staggered a few steps before he collapsed in the street. "*That* racket, Timberlaine! You deaf or what?"

Timberlaine looked at the unconscious cowhand and shrugged.

"Some of the boys are celebratin', that's all, Sheriff. Halliday's out to break Tom Meisner's record of—"

"Halliday!"

The name exploded from Lomar's lips.

"Yeah, Sheriff. I've seen some of the best, but when Halliday sets himself to—"

Lomar shoved Timberlaine aside and snapped, "Come with me, mister! We'll see how far that damned drifter thinks he can go in my town. Judas, it's been four or five times now that I've warned him about ..."

The rest of Lomar's outburst was drowned by the crash of bodies inside the batwings, then three cowhands came flying out through the swing doors to knock Lomar aside. One of the batwings was torn off a hinge and the window on that side of the wall shattered into tiny fragments. As Lomar went down under flailing arms and legs, his angry shouts of protest were drowned by the arrival, on the seat of his pants, of a fourth cowhand, who laid him out completely.

Timberlaine glanced down at Lomar, who lay there momentarily stunned, then he made a quick exit down the alley beside the saloon. From inside, more noise broke out.

Finally, Lomar scrambled to his feet, planted a right on the jaw of a tall, skin-and-bone cowhand and sent him staggering into the wall. Encouraged, Lomar straightened his gunbelt, drove the holster down to its correct position on his hip, and whipped out his gun. When he burst through the batwings, kicking broken chairs and glass out of his way, he saw Halliday grappling with the combined weight of four cowhands.

Lomar stopped dead in his tracks, his face scarlet with rage, his gun lifting. But then, seeing Halliday's head jolt back from a solid punch, he kept his gun hand still and watched.

A wide-shouldered, thick-chested man of better than medium height, Halliday suddenly cut loose, throwing punches in all directions. Lomar swore when two of Halliday's adversaries went down hard, and a third, lifted off the floor by a powerful Halliday arm, kicked out frantically until Halliday hurled him away. The cowhand's boot struck Lomar on the forearm and jolted the gun from his hand. While he was cursing and scrabbling about on the floor for it, Halliday caught sight of him.

9

So did the fourth cowhand, as he charged straight at Halliday. So did the crowd of onlookers, in whose eyes all excitement suddenly died when somebody yelled;

"Hell, it's Lomar!"

There was a moment of silence and inactivity before a dozen men made themselves busy at the counter. Wiping blood from his mouth, Halliday walked lazily back to the counter and picked up his unfinished drink. He was sipping at it when Lomar barked;

"Halliday! Don't you move a step, dammit! Don't even blink. You've gone too far this time!"

The lawman came striding across the room, his gun in his hand again and his face flushed with anger. He shouldered two townsmen aside, kicked a dazed cowhand in the seat of the pants and palmed another bloody-faced cowpuncher out of his way. His mouth was no more than an ugly slash in his pinched, drawn face, when he snarled;

"Now, you upstart, we can get down to dealin' with you. I told you a dozen times that while you're in my town you'll have to mind your manners!"

"I've been doin' that, Sheriff," Halliday said calmly, trying not to laugh.

Lomar's eyebrows arched. He waved his hand about, a gesture that covered the four corners of the room. "You have, you say? Then what the hell do you call *this* ... a gatherin' of Ma Briller's sewing circle?"

Halliday took a moment to gaze around the room. He pursed his lips thoughtfully and then the beginning of a smile caught at the corners of his mouth. "Seems there's been a power of needlin' done, Sheriff, I'll allow."

Lomar drew in a ragged breath, making it plain to the onlookers that he was losing his struggle to keep his temper in check. He kept moving his gun up and down in front of his lithe, lean body, while his rage held hard. Halliday then realized he may have gone too far, and said quietly;

"In a nutshell, Sheriff, what started out as a bit of fun kinda got out of hand. But it wasn't my fault."

"I'll back that up, Lomar," said a runt of a cowhand who was still wiping blood from a gashed eyebrow and looking for all the world like he'd gone three rounds with a bull in a stable. "Guess you remember me. Tim Shelvy from the Bar-Nine Ranch. A few of the boys dared Halliday to have a go at Tom Meisner's record, which we figure has stood for way too long. Halliday put up his money and then he set himself down and the drinks kept comin'. Damn me if he didn't look a sitter to beat Tom's record. Then Bobby Meisner, who ain't never been a good loser, started to bait Halliday and finally said somethin' which got Halliday's dander up. So Halliday hit him to shut him up. That would have been it, I reckon, if Bobby's brother, Poke, hadn't arrived just in time to see Bobby go down. Poke got the wrong slant on things, I reckon, and went for Halliday, who hit him with an uppercut that put Poke in Charlie Monday's lap and broke Charlie's best pipe. Charlie just had to get even, so he started swingin'. Then I got hit. After that, an' I don't rightly know how, we were all in it. I guess most of us just natcherly went for Halliday, prob'ly 'cause we reckoned he'd started the whole thing. Only he didn't, not when you stop to think about it."

Shelvy looked about him and a number of heads nodded in agreement. Bracing himself against the counter in the face of Lomar's withering stare, he went on;

"Halliday stood his ground an' he was beatin' the stuffin' out of some of us when we decided to rush him. That was when he really got mean, and started hurlin' some of us through the door and out the winders."

12

Shelvy shook his head as if unable to believe what had happened.

"That's when you came in, Sheriff. We didn't see you right off, and I guess you kinda got in the way. But, hell, it wasn't nothin' more'n I've told you, some of the boys letting off a little steam, on account things have been real quiet around here of late and—"

"*Quiet?*" Lomar boomed. "What the hell kind of bulldust are you feedin' me now? A man ain't been able to close one eye let alone two since you and Halliday set your butts down in here!"

Most of the crowd had discreetly sidled away, leaving Shelvy and Halliday alone at the counter to face the music. Even the barkeep had gone off to sweep the fragments of glass up from the floor near the front window.

"We tried our best to be orderly, Sheriff," Shelvy said quietly, but with little assurance in his voice. "It's like I said, things got a little outta hand and, well, you know how it is when hard-workin' men find they've got time on their hands and money in their pockets—"

"Shut up, damn you!" Lomar roared.

He took hold of Shelvy and hurled him at a group of cowhands who were to a man nursing cuts and bruises. Lomar then turned to Halliday

13

again, his forefinger punching holes in the whiskey-tainted air between them.

"As for you, you're through in this town. I've taken all I'm gonna take from you, and I don't give a hoot whether you're in the right or the wrong. Where you are, that's where trouble is, every damn minute of every damn day and every damn night! So saddle up and ride, and keep ridin' and don't never come back."

Halliday slowly straightened, holding Lomar's stern gaze in his own. He was tempted to tell the lawman to go to hell, but in a way, he realized the predicament he'd put the man in. For four days now, he and the Bar-Nine bunch had been drinking solidly, and only that morning he'd decided that he'd had enough.

The call of the trail beckoned him, and his feet were getting restless.

"I'll be gone come sundown, Sheriff," Halliday told him.

"You'll be gone come ten minutes, mister!" Lomar roared. "If you ain't, you can spend the night in a cell."

Shelvy was about to protest when Lomar swung on him. "You, too, cowboy! If you say one more word, I'll put bars between us. Just get these jaspers packed together and finish your drinkin'.

Then get to hell home and do some work for a change. This whole damn town is sick and tired of you."

"I'm not, Sheriff Lomar," said a husky female voice from the curtained doorway leading to the rooms in back.

Lomar turned as a woman in her late thirties shimmied toward him. She was tall and slim and looked completely composed. Her eyes took in the room, showing no resentment as she eyed the wreckage.

"You stay outta this, Lucy," Lomar said harshly. "Do that and I'll see that this bunch pays you for the damage done. Judas, I'm not gonna let a single one of 'em get away with it this time!"

"They'll pay me nothing, Sheriff Lomar," Lucy said quietly. She was cool and serene, but there was a hint of fire and fury in her eyes. "They're my customers and I'm indebted to them for their business. I think I'll be able to tidy up the place so it won't have to close while repairs are carried out, and I'm sure I can do without your assistance."

Lomar again went red in the face. "Judas ..." he began, but Lucy gestured for him to be silent and told the barkeep to fill the glasses lined up on the counter. Then she took Lomar's arm.

"Ted, you do allow your temper to get the better of you sometimes," Lucy said gently. "It's been awful hot today and tomorrow might be worse. So let's just have a drink and forget that somebody spoiled your nap."

Lomar was against the counter before he pulled away from her, muttering a curse as he heard a snicker from one of the cowhands. His glare sought out the offender but the men were already jostling each other to get to the counter.

"Dammit, Lucy—" Lomar started to say, before a shot rang out from the Red Garter opposite.

Lomar spun on his heel, the redness gone from his face. Glass in hand, Lucy said;

"At least nobody here started *that*, Ted. Perhaps you should check it out, seeing as how ours has been settled to everyone's satisfaction. The boys were just about done, anyway."

Lomar stepped away from her, his teeth bared, then he turned to Halliday and snapped, "What I said still goes, mister! Git and don't come back."

Halliday's face was expressionless. Lomar grunted, then strode across the room, shouldering drinkers out of his way. He paused in the doorway to study the wreckage, then he pulled the broken batwing off its one hinge and hurled it into the room.

Cussing a blue streak, he went straight across the street, gun out, and came to a halt on the edge of the Red Garter's boardwalk. The echo of the gunshot had long since faded and a deep silence had settled on the place.

Lomar waited, expecting something further to happen. When the silence persisted, he strode toward the batwings. He had his left hand on the top of one swing door when a tall man dressed in black and wearing twin gunbelts approached him from the depths of the saloon.

The man stopped and his stare took the lawman in carefully before he stepped past him and strode confidently to a horse tethered at the hitch rack. Lomar was of a mind to stop him when there was a sudden tattoo of hoof beats from the alley alongside the saloon. Then came a frightened cry and an old man came running from the alley to hotfoot it across the boardwalk.

Not knowing where to look next, Lomar stood rooted to the warped boards while the old man faltered on the edge of the boardwalk and had to grab for an overhang post to stop himself from falling. Then bullets began to gouge the boards and the dusty street itself.

The shooters turned out to be a bunch of riders who came thundering out of the alley and continued to shoot up the ground around the old man's feet. The oldster let out another frantic cry, grabbed at his left ankle and limped into the street, looking desperately about him. It was then that Lomar called;

"You there, hold it! That's enough!"

A few of the riders looked his way, but the bulk of the bunch kept after the old man, circling him and keeping him penned like a frightened steer. The old man, white-faced and scared out of his wits, finally dropped to the ground. Lomar then saw blood seeping out of the toe of his left boot.

The sheriff then put three shots across the heads of the riders. The echoes of his gunshots were dying when a horse loomed up on his left. The sweat-flecked shoulder of the animal hit him in the back and sent him sprawling to the dust.

Lomar tried to rise but pain exploded in his head and his vision became blurry. He thought he saw a woman, waving her hands excitedly about and shouting. He also thought he saw Halliday and the Bar-Nine bunch leaving Lovely Lucy's saloon. He gritted his teeth and rubbed at eyes that were filled with grit. He knelt there, powerless to do anything but cuss, anger mounting inside him.

Buck Halliday was first to reach the boardwalk of the Lovely Lucy. He was two long strides ahead of Tim Shelvy and the Bar-Nine crew. They stood on either side of him, watching the ruckus in the street. When Halliday saw a slim young woman running straight toward the milling horses, he said;

"Who are those rannies, Tim?"

"Latimer's bunch." Shelvy frowned. "Them and us aren't exactly on speakin' terms."

"Latimer?" Halliday pressed.

"Aldo Latimer. The big feller, that's Zac Whelan." Shelvy rubbed a hand across the point of his jaw. "I got a real good reason to remember that ranny."

The young woman was only yards away from the riders when Halliday noticed the whip in her hand. He stepped toward her, and when she ducked under the head of one of the lead horses and reached down to help the old man to his feet, he broke into a run.

Two riders saw him coming and scowled, then they looked past him to the Bar-Nine crew.

"The odds are a little one-sided, mister," Halliday said to the closest rider.

When the man's gun pointed down at him, he threw himself to the side and grabbed the rider's wrist. With a jerk, he pulled the cowboy from the saddle. He then slapped the horse on the rump and ducked under the neck of a second horse. A bullet buzzed past his face and he twisted and caught the rider by the shirtfront and hauled him from the saddle. They went to the ground together and rolled, before Halliday came up on top of his man. He looked down at a face fast filling with fear, and then his fists pistoned out in short, sharp punches. The cowhand kicked and squirmed before Halliday landed a full-blooded right squarely on the man's mouth. Teeth broke and blood spurted and the man's head lolled to the side.

Then more bullets ripped into the ground beside Halliday's leg.

He sprang to his feet and locked eyes on the big man Shelvy had pointed out to him—Zac Whelan, tubby, broad-shouldered and swarthy-skinned. Then Halliday caught sight of the woman.

She stood with her feet planted and her slim body jerking this way and that as she lashed out with her whip. The whip cut a man's face and sent him staggering away and clawing at his eyes. The woman stood her ground, keeping a hand on the old man's forearm while she lashed out with her whip again, perfectly willing to take them all on if she had to.

Shelvy went down and Halliday wanted to run to help him, but there was no time. Whelan was leering down at him, clubbing at Halliday's head with the butt of his gun.

Halliday dodged the blows, reached out and got a hold on Whelan's leg and dragged him from the saddle. Whelan's body hit the ground with a loud thud and air exploded from his lungs. The lash of the woman's whip and the cries of Latimer's riders were now all that Halliday could hear. For now the shooting had stopped. Through the corner of his eye, he saw Latimer's men begin to gain the upper hand.

Whelan clawed his way to his feet, still full of fight. Halliday took a painful blow on the shoulder, rode the next punch in an attempt to get in close. He was all business now, the man of a hundred fistfights, the drifter who was locking horns with a man twice his size. He had no help and needed none. He stood alone and that was the way he liked it. His fists lashed out, drumming into Whelan's big face with terrible impact, mauling and hurting and sapping the big man's strength. Whelan stood there and took the punishment, shocked to the soles of his boots before his hands slowly dropped to his sides.

Halliday kept punching away at him, but Whelan refused to go down. Then, suddenly, the big man began to falter. He could take no more. His knees buckled and he stared blearily at his attacker, his bruised and swollen face rutted with pain and disbelief. His mouth hung slack. Halliday sucked down a deep breath and measured his man, then mercifully hooked a solid right to the point of Whelan's jaw. The big man's eyes rolled in their sockets before he collapsed to the ground, out cold.

Dust was settling as Halliday turned to survey the scene. Shelvy and the Bar-Nine crew held the Latimer bunch at bay with cocked six-guns, and the young woman ran down the boardwalk to an old rig.

She got quickly into the driver's seat and drove it beside the old man and jumped down. Halliday watched her help the oldster into the rig and then scramble back onto the seat. She looked back once and caught his eye.

Something approaching gratitude burned in those eyes for a moment, then she lashed the whip across the horse's rump and the rig rolled away, stirring up more dust that screened her departure. When she'd gone, Tim Shelvy said;

"Over here, Halliday. Leave 'em where they are."

Halliday calmly looked Shelvy's way. Ted Lomar was on his feet, still rubbing at his eyes. When he saw Halliday, his mouth opened and he would have spoken if the tall man in black wearing the double gunbelt hadn't emerged from the alley beside the Red Garter. He stepped neatly into the saddle and peered darkly at Halliday, until Lomar said;

"It's over, Mann. Finito. Your men started this and weren't up to finishin' it. If there's to be anymore gunplay, the first bullet better go through me."

Mann gave Lomar a look of pure contempt before returning his gaze to Halliday. "Who are you?"

"Who's askin'?"

"Rees Mann. You?"

"Halliday."

"It's a name I won't forget, mister," Mann said, then he heeled his horse toward the Latimer bunch.

They were bruised and beaten and sullenly silent. He spoke to them in a soft voice and they moved off to collect their injured friends. It took two of them to get Zac Whelan to his feet and help him onto his horse. Even then one man had to ride at the big man's side to keep him in the saddle. Mann led them away, but at the street's end, he turned and looked back.

The stare he gave Halliday was loaded with hate. It was obvious to Halliday that the man meant what he said.

TWO

"GET, AND STAY OUT!"

"No, Shelvy, hold it there!" Sheriff Ted Lomar said as he moved across Tim Shelvy's path to plant a hand against his chest. "You ain't goin' no place just yet."

"Why not? Dammit, Sheriff, don't start preachin' to me. You busted in on that ruckus and got yourself in a heap o' trouble. We saw you go down and then we bought in so you wouldn't get your fool head stoved in."

"I don't know why you bought in, mister, and I don't care," Lomar scowled. "Latimer's bunch have headed home, and since you'll be goin' in the same direction, I don't want you two groups usin' the trail at the same time. You'll wait here and you won't leave town till well after dark."

Tim Shelvy, whose thirst had returned with a vengeance, shrugged his weary shoulders and muttered, "Well, if that's the way you want it, Sheriff, sure, we'll stay. Halliday, you feel like another drink?"

"Halliday don't feel like doin' nothin' 'cept puttin' his butt in a saddle and headin' north."

"Why north, Sheriff?" Halliday asked calmly.

"Because you'll travel faster if you head north. I'm rememberin' what you told me when you arrived—that you were on the drift, lookin' for work and didn't give a damn where you went or why. So you take the north trail and get to hell outta my sight and stay out of it!"

Halliday wiped his knuckles down his shirt-front and stepped past Lomar to wash up in the street's water trough. Waving his hands about to dry them, he gave Lomar an easy smile.

"Sheriff, I just want to tell you I've thoroughly enjoyed myself in your town and I'm indebted to you more than anybody else for that. If it hadn't been for you, I don't reckon that me or the boys here would have got so much kick out of today. Fact is, I'm so grateful that I want to shake your hand."

Lomar frowned heavily and looked down at Halliday's extended arm. Then his gaze swung up and took in the faces of Shelvy and the other Bar-Nine cowhands. Their serious looks fooled Lomar into nodding at Halliday and taking his hand. But almost immediately a roar of laughter came from Shelvy and he stepped forward and slapped Halliday on the back.

"Halliday, by hell, you're a card, ain't you? Damn me, but don't you drag the limit out of everythin'. I got to buy you one last drink, by hell, right now!"

Lomar realized he'd again been made look a fool. He drew his gun, shoved Shelvy aside with his shoulder and drove the gun into Halliday's middle.

"Git!" Lomar roared. "Now!"

Halliday gave the lawman a slow smile. "No need for that, Sheriff. I'll go ... but in my own time."

"Just so you go," Lomar threw back at him, but something sharp in Halliday's voice made him put the gun away.

Halliday went to his horse and checked to see that it hadn't been harmed during the ruckus before he climbed into the saddle. He pulled his hat slightly down over his eyes and looked about him.

Duke Timberlaine was standing outside the Lovely Lucy, leaning against the wall. A cigarette hung loosely from his lips and his eyes danced with amusement. Lucy was beside him, looking straight at Halliday, disappointment in her eyes.

"Thanks for the hospitality, ma'am," Halliday called to her, then he dug a gold coin from his pocket and flipped it toward her. "For my share of the damage," he added and turned his sorrel away.

Lucy caught the coin deftly. She dropped it between the hollow of her breasts and called, "Come back soon, Buck. You're always mighty welcome."

"Just might do that," Halliday said, ignoring Lomar's ferocious scowl. He heeled the sorrel to Tim Shelvy and touched the brim of his hat. "See you 'round."

"You can always find us at the Bar-Nine, Halliday," Shelvy said. "Wouldn't worry us none if you happened to drop by some time."

Halliday nodded, and then looking straight along the south trail, smiled and touched his horse into a run. The sorrel responded immediately and settled into an easy lope ... north.

Moving into the street again, Lomar wiped a hand across his sweating face and breathed a deep sigh of relief. Then he turned and made his way back to the jailhouse. But even after he had dropped into his boardwalk chair and adjusted his hat so he could see as much as he wanted under the eye-shading brim, he was still frowning. It had been a close call, he told himself, that Latimer mob and the Bar-Nine excitement-hungry cowpunchers locking horns, not to mention Halliday up to his ears in the thick of it. A real close thing, and something he might not have been able to handle. Still, he consoled himself, it was over now. The Latimer bunch had gone home and Halliday had ridden out in the other direction. All that remained to worry this lawman was a bunch of men taking on board more whiskey than they could possibly handle. But that, he reminded himself, was not all that unusual.

It was a winding trail that led north out of Cannon Creek. Halliday rode it slowly after the town had gone from sight. He enjoyed the freshness of the evening air and was trying to make up his mind how far he would ride before he camped for the night, when he saw vague shapes ahead.

He didn't bother to draw rein. The sorrel kept on, picking its way through the gloom. There was no moon yet, but the sky was clear and coming alive with stars. The earthy smell of the country-side filled his nostrils, fingering his senses like hands on piano keys. He felt good, despite the shapes ahead that might not be friendly.

"You've just come from Cannon Creek?" a woman called out to him.

Halliday stopped the sorrel. A rig's outline was clear enough, and soon the woman took shape, her hair brushed back from her face, her head held high.

"Yes, I came from Cannon Creek."

"Are you the man who helped us in the street?"

Halliday rode his horse side-on to the rig. The light was a little better on this high, treeless section of trail, but not strong enough for him to make out her features properly. But his mind went over the picture she had made getting into the rig in town, her skirt flying and her long legs flashing.

"If you were that woman, then I guess I could've been some help to you."

There was a moment's quiet between them, then the young woman stared anxiously into the back of the rig, and said;

"My name is Hope Clayton. My uncle is in the back. He's hurt badly, I think. We're very grateful to you, Mr. …?"

"Halliday, ma'am. Buck Halliday."

"Mr. Halliday," she went on, "a few miles back I saw you and thought you looked like the man who helped us. My uncle wanted me to invite you home. He wants you to stay the night so he can speak to you in the morning."

"Where's home, ma'am?" Halliday asked.

"This way," she said, pointing with the whip the way to a trail through humpbacked hills, the trail just wide enough to take a rig.

"Our place is about a mile from here, in a small valley."

Halliday nodded and said, "What would your uncle want to speak to me about, ma'am?"

"Maybe he just wants to thank you … he's very grateful." Her voice had an edge of worry to it.

Halliday looked more intently about him, but all that showed was a gash in the hills and dark blobs of foliage. Yet there was a buzz of warning in his head. It was no more than a hunch, but he had the feeling that spending the night with this woman and her uncle might only mean further trouble.

"Ma'am, when your uncle comes to," Halliday said, "you tell him that he's not beholden to me. Fact is, the men I was with would have taken on that bunch if I hadn't been there. Seems there's no love lost between those two outfits."

"Do you know who they were?" Hope asked, peering intently at him and looking more worried now.

"I didn't know until the fight was over and you were on your way out of town, ma'am. I don't even know which outfit was in the right, or why those men were gangin' up against your uncle."

He saw her lips pinch tight and her grip tighten on the whip. Then she drew in a deep breath and he saw the outline of her bosom straining against her blouse.

"Do you have a place to go?" Hope asked.

"No, ma'am. I'm a drifter—"

"My uncle said you looked like a drifter," Hope said with amazement in her voice. "I have no idea how he knew. He said you had the look of a man who likes to keep on the move. Which means you're probably in no great hurry to get anywhere, Mr. Halliday. Am I right in assuming that?"

"Look," Halliday went on, speaking quietly and leaning forward in the saddle so he could see her eyes more clearly, "I helped you out in town, ma'am. That doesn't make you indebted to me. In fact, I enjoyed myself, now that I come to think about it. So you and your uncle don't owe me anymore than a word of thanks, which you've just given me. So, if you head home, I'll just keep ridin'."

The woman took a deep breath and Halliday thought he saw a tear come to her eye when she said;

"As you wish, but we're merely offering you a bed and a meal, Mr. Halliday. My uncle thought it was little enough we could do to repay you. But never mind, and thank you again. Good night."

She flicked the whip across the back of the horse and headed it for the gash of trail between the two hills.

Halliday kept the sorrel in check, watching her go. Dammit, he told himself, all he'd done was get a little drunk, tangle with a bunch of cowhands who'd had too much to drink and who worked for a man named Latimer. Then he had locked horns with a lawman, got booted out of town with plenty of bruises on his face, shoulders and body. Anything else apart from all that was none of his business, and making it his business could so easily mean trouble.

And for what …?

The rig was almost out of sight when Halliday heeled the sorrel after it and pulled on the horse's headstall to pull it up. Then he rode back to the rig and said;

"How bad's your uncle hurt, ma'am?"

"Bad enough. He's lost a lot of blood. And the town doctor was called out to the Johnston family to deliver their firstborn. Uncle was in such terrible pain that soon after he saw you, he passed out."

Halliday looked ahead. "Then maybe you'll need some help to get him into the house, ma'am. How far to your place, did you say?"

"Just over a mile."

"Well, I guess that ain't far outta my way, ma'am. So if you'll lead the way, I'll tag along."

She lifted a hand to wipe away the tear. She bit her lip, gave him a nod and slapped her horse on again.

They followed the trail for a half-mile or so then the rig turned sharply right to take a trail that dropped quickly into a small valley. Here the air had a cold bite to it, and the smell of grass and pines bit the back of Halliday's nostrils. Another quarter of a mile on, he made out the faint outline of a cabin.

During the drive, he began to wonder why a woman and an old man would want to settle out here, far from the comforts of town and the protection of the law. It was often dangerous in wilderness like this.

Some drifters weren't beyond taking what they wanted from a defenseless woman—which made him curious as to why she trusted him enough to invite him back to her home, not knowing anything more about him other than he was a man who enjoyed a brawl.

The woman drew the rig up outside the small cabin. The moon was out and Halliday could see that the garden before it was clean and neat.

The woman spent some time unlatching the twin locks on the door. Why they had gone to all that trouble of attaching twin locks when a gun butt could so easily smash in a window, amused him.

After a moment, lantern light poured through the open doorway. Halliday hitched his sorrel to the rack and walked to the rig. He stared in at the huddled figure in back, seeing the old, lined face clearly in the moonlight.

"What do you think?" Hope asked at his side.

He was aware now of how worried she looked.

"Hard to say, out here. His bunk ready?"

"Yes."

"Then I'll carry him inside."

The woman pulled off the old man's boots and held the lantern high so Halliday could see the way. He carried the old-timer inside and was amazed how light he felt. Then he gently lowered the oldster to a bunk and undid the buttons of his shirt, exposing his sunken chest. The fact that the old man had long been unable to do hard work was clearly evident. As Halliday stepped away to let the woman look at him, he wondered who kept the yard and garden so neat and orderly.

He studied the young woman closely. She was reed-slender, but her tight riding skirt showed firm, shapely hips and the strain of the blouse across her bosom told of the size of her breasts. He found her looking suddenly at him, her long-lashed eyes candidly appraising him.

"He's lost a lot of blood," she said. "Will you watch him while I put some water on the stove. I have a medicine chest with some bandages and liniment. If he gets a good night's rest, he'll be all right in the morning."

Cool. Calm. Perhaps she was accustomed to emergencies like this.

Halliday leaned against the wall and fashioned a smoke. While he smoked he watched her— assured and confident in everything she did. Halliday couldn't help but notice how gentle she was with the old man, striving to spare him pain while she did what had to be done with his bullet wound. When she was finished, she breathed a sigh of relief, then smiled at Halliday.

"I can't do anymore for him now. His breathing is normal and I can see color returning to his cheeks. It's a terrible thing when an old man who's worked hard all his life can't live out his remaining days in peace."

Halliday held his tongue. She fussed awhile longer at the bedside before she crossed the room and busied herself at the stove. Halliday thought about leaving. He'd done what was asked of him, so what was there to keep him here?

Yet he kept looking at her, admiring her self-assurance. Here, he told himself, was some woman, one any man would be proud to know. The lamplight on her face showed how beautiful she was despite the strain she was under.

Halliday pinched out his cigarette and flicked the butt out the open door. When she brought him coffee and a plate of stew, he smiled at her and sat down at the table.

His two-day drinking bout with Tim Shelvy and his crew had left little time for eating. Suddenly, he realized how hungry he was, and he attacked the stew with a gusto that brought a smile to her lips.

"I can see you enjoy your food as much as you say you enjoy a good fight, Mr. Halliday. It's good to see that in a man. My uncle annoys me the way he picks at his food. Sometimes it makes me think I'm not so good a cook."

"That," Halliday said, indicating the empty plate with his fork, "was delicious, ma'am."

"I'm so pleased you like it," she said, and brought the pot from the stove to the table.

Ignoring Halliday's halfhearted protests, she filled his plate again. Then remembering the many trails he'd ridden with the lining of his stomach as flat as a sun-cured pelt, he set about eating again.

While he ate, the woman went about tidying the room that was already free from dust. Halliday had the feeling she was merely filling in time. He then couldn't help but wonder again what they were doing out here.

The valley seemed fertile enough, but could a woman and an old man eke out a living here? It was certainly not big enough to run a good-sized herd, and the country beyond it as he rode in looked nothing but desert and rocky hills.

He had just pushed the empty plate away when she stopped before him and looked at him intently. She seemed on the verge of saying something, then she shrugged and turned away.

"What's troublin' you, ma'am?"

She looked back at him and her lips quivered. "I have no right to ask. The meal was little enough in payment for what you've done."

"You seemed to be worried about somethin' more than your uncle's condition," Halliday said, and noticed the quick rise of her eyebrows. "How about tellin' me?"

She wrung her hands and looked through the window at the clearing. The moonlight was stronger now. "They might come tonight," she said in a voice that was no more than a whisper.

"They?"

"Latimer and his hired killers."

It was Halliday's turn to raise an eyebrow. He watched the color drain from her face and knew that fear had taken hold of her. He pushed out a chair for her and asked her to sit down. When she was seated, her shoulders slumped and her hands rested nervously on the tabletop. Then Halliday said;

"The beginning is always the best place to start, ma'am."

She nodded and he saw tears form in her eyes again. But she bravely fought them away, drew in a deep sigh and said;

"Latimer first came to visit us six months ago. He offered to buy us out … and for a good price, or to exchange it for a bigger and better place closer to town, with a fine house thrown in. I was so excited that I told him I'd talk to my uncle when he returned. Latimer said he was expanding his interests and he'd like an answer within three days, or he'd have to bypass us and make an offer to some of our neighbors."

"Do you and your uncle have joint claim on this property, ma'am?" Halliday asked.

"Yes. My father and Uncle Dick worked a few head of cattle in this area in the old days. Then they discovered a little hidden-away section and filed a claim on it. When pa died, he willed his share to me, but naturally I always listen to what Uncle Dick says."

"And your uncle didn't want to do business with Latimer?" Halliday pressed.

The woman nodded.

"He felt the offer was too good to be true. He wanted to know why Latimer was so keen to buy us out, so he went to town and started asking questions. That was when the trouble started."

"Why should that be?"

"We don't know," Hope admitted. "At first it was nothing Uncle Dick could put his finger on. Little things ... a wheel nut loosened on the rig which might have caused some terrible injury if he hadn't noticed it before leaving town. Then there were the men riding the rim of the hills, always riding off when Uncle Dick went up to speak to them and ask why they were trespassing on our land. Then Latimer made a second visit. He was the thorough gentleman, full of compliments and praise for what we've done out here. Once again he insisted that his time was short. Uncle Dick asked him more questions and Latimer got very evasive. Although he still insisted that he could buy land elsewhere, he seemed terribly put out when Uncle Dick said he needed time to think about it. Then the water in our well was salted."

Halliday straightened. Like every range man, he considered the salting of drinking water to be a crime almost equal to murder. "How bad was it salted?"

Hope shook her head. "I don't know all that much about such things, Mr. Halliday. I made Uncle Dick his usual cup of coffee first thing in the morning. He almost threw up. He made a thorough check and discovered that the spring had been heavily salted at its source. He said it would take some heavy rain to wash the salt away, and if we'd had cattle drinking that water we would be in terrible trouble."

Halliday began to build another cigarette. Getting back on the trail no longer appealed to him as strongly as it had. He was about to ask her about Latimer's next move when the old man stirred on the bunk. Looking that way, he saw the oldster lifting his head from the pillows. Then he looked around the room, saw the newcomer and said in a weak voice;

"H-Halliday, ain't it?"

Halliday nodded and the old man worked himself into a more comfortable position.

"Figgered it was you I saw in town when those scum were havin' their fun with me. Heard all about you before that, kickin' up your heels and annoyin' the hell outta Ted Lomar, which, in my opinion, ain't a crime." The old man voice was strong, and he showed no sign that his foot was worrying him all that much. "Then, when I seen somebody trailin' us from town, I prayed it was you. A man helps a feller out once, it could mean he won't mind helpin' him out again."

When Halliday didn't respond, the woman walked across the room and tried to fuss over her uncle again, but he eased her aside and went on;

"I just been listenin' to what my girl's been tellin' you, Halliday. She has it right as far as she went, but that ain't the half of it. Latimer's a troublemaker. He's got an bunch o' killers on his payroll, led by a black-eyed, black-hearted gun-fighter named Rees Mann. Did you see him in town a-tall?"

"The man in black, double guns?" Halliday asked.

"That's the varmint. Thinks he's top man 'round here, the way he struts. But so help me, nobody, not Latimer nor his roughhouse ram-rod, Zac Whelan, and not even Rees Mann, is gonna tell me to git when I don't want to."

"Uncle Dick," Hope put in anxiously, "you shouldn't excite yourself so much. You've been hurt and you need—"

"What I need, girl, is a gun in my hand and them scum in my sights. Hell, I only pretended to be drunk today. Yet I stood up to the whole bunch—and I did it for a reason—I wanted to know how far they'd go. Well, I found out. They didn't do much more'n shoot up the ground under my feet but Mann made it clear enough that next time it'll be Boothill for me and God knows what for you. Still, I ain't givin' this place up, not after what I learned yesterday and had confirmed today."

"Which was?" Halliday asked, sensing the old-timer was at last about to get to the core of the

43

whole thing. He noticed then that Hope was confused, perhaps even as much as he was. The old man said;

"Son, I feel I can trust you. The story is, a railroad company is plannin' to build a spur line through to Cannon Creek. They reckon the cheapest way for them to go is straight across the desert and then cut through the mountains. That way, although the construction costs will be higher, they don't have to pay for good grazin' land. What land they want they can get just by layin' claim to it." His old eyes sparkled with amusement and he chuckled, sitting forward. "Our land, Halliday, sits right in their way. Latimer somehow got wind of the company's plans, so natcherly he tried to cheat me and Hope out of what's legally ours. He ain't gonna do it, though, not while I got teeth enough to chew a cud with."

Hope stood just short of the bed and gaped at her uncle. "Do you mean our land is—?"

"Worth a fortune, girl. I got it on good authority that the railroad ain't out to cheat nobody and they already know about our valley and how important it is to their plans. They're willin' to pay us what it's worth to them rather than what it's worth to us." Hope frowned and looked at

Halliday. "How long do we have to hold out, do you think, Uncle?"

"A week, girl, no more. I sent word for one of the railroad representatives to get out here as fast as he can and we'll sign the place over to him. All we gotta do is hold Latimer's bunch off till then—and that's where Halliday comes in."

"Just where *do* I come in, old-timer?" Halliday asked.

The old man grinned at Halliday and pointed at the floor at the side of the bed. "Here, Halliday. I know just enough about you to realize you're footloose and fancy free and ain't agin takin' a gamble. Also, you're tough, and you've got the kinda guts a job like this needs. Yep, you're a man who ain't scared of the whine of a bullet or two. So I'm glad you accepted our invitation to come here and now here's my offer, straight off the cuff."

Through the corner of his eye Halliday saw fear spread across Hope's pretty face. Without a doubt, the old man had all the say in this partnership. He was a smart one, and no mistake. Smart and slick.

Maybe too slick …?

"My offer, Halliday, is five hundred dollars, cash on the barrelhead for one week's work. All you gotta do is stand guard back at the pass. You already came through there and you can see how easy it would be to hold off a bunch of gun tippers intent on gettin' through. Two, three days from now and I'll be up and about to help. I guarantee that not a damned one of them will get through to this place. After they get tired of being shot at, we can sneak off in the night and do some signin' and get me and Hope all the money that belongs to us. Then we'll pay you and you can go on your way."

Halliday did some quick thinking. His funds were running low after all the excitement at Cannon Creek, and his body could do with some work. But he wasn't sure that it was work of this kind. In the back of his mind was the knowledge that Tim Shelvy and the Bar-Nine crew were companionable types once you got to know them. And because they hated the Latimer bunch's guts, didn't it fall into place that Latimer was all Dick Clayton claimed him to be, and maybe more?

Hope had crossed the room to stand at her uncle's side. Now he held her arm and spoke in a whisper that Halliday couldn't hear. He saw Hope stiffen and shake her head. Then the oldster motioned her away and said;

"All right, Halliday, what's it to be? You've got only an old man and a slip of a girl to help you, but you've got a fortress about you. I saw you walk into trouble with the spirit of a man who doesn't mind gettin' his hands dirty and maybe stung by a few bullets. Five hundred dollars, Halliday, for a week's work and dinin' on Hope's cookin'. I'll want your answer now, right this minute, 'cause if you aim to ride away, then get it done so Hope can help me get up to that pass. I'll hold off that miserable bunch on my lonesome."

Halliday wiped a hand across his brow and was surprised to find a line of sweat there. Hope had gone to the far corner of the room and seemed occupied with thoughts of her own. In the dark, her features were in shadow. He wanted to see her expression, to delve deep into her thoughts. He felt that in her lay the answer to the question of what he should do. Then the old man was talking again.

"If it'll help, Halliday, and I ain't just sayin' it 'cause I'm down on my luck, I want you to remember what happened in town. Hope took to them buzzards with her whip and left some scars on some of 'em which they ain't likely to forget in a hurry. If you go, you'll be leavin' us to fight 'em alone, and mebbe the two of us ain't up to the challenge. If they get through that pass, they'll kill me and then they'll have Hope to do with as they want. When you're ridin' away, mister, you think on that, on what will happen to her, a girl who ain't done no harm to anybody in her whole life."

Halliday swore under his breath. Hope took a step toward her uncle that brought her face into the light. There was the shine of anger in her eyes and her face was tight with resentment. But the cunning oldster had said his piece, and now he looked at Halliday, his gaze defiant, demanding.

"When do you expect they'll come?" Halliday asked.

"Tonight. I know Latimer. And I know how far I've pushed him and his no-good bunch. This is the end of the line, Halliday. It's showdown time. So either you ride back to guard that pass and help us or you ride through it on your way out, knowin' full well what'll happen to us."

Hope had her mouth open to speak when her uncle pulled on her skirt.

"While he's decidin', you'd best take a look at my ankle. All this talk's set it to throbbin'. Feels to me like the bone's broke."

Halliday got to his feet and went to the doorway. He stood there, hearing the girl's skirt swishing as she made her way across the room.

Why in hell did he allow himself to get caught up in other people's troubles?

He stepped into a night where only the chirping of crickets disturbed the silence. He stood there, broad shoulders brushing the timber. His face was set hard and his eyes made a cool, searching appraisal of the clearing and the grassed valley slopes beyond. He went back to the door and said;

"All right," and stepped down from the porch.

As he moved toward his sorrel, he heard the girl moving about in the cabin but then her uncle said something to her and all movement ceased.

Halliday stepped up into the saddle and checked his gun. His stomach was full, but his throat was dry.

What the heck, he thought, Lomar had stopped the ruckus in town just as he was getting up a man-sized thirst …

THREE

SOMEBODY'S MISTAKE

Buck Halliday had met Dick Clayton's kind before. More often than not, behind the bluster of words and the show of false bravado, was a man with a heart of gold who would give you the shirt off his back.

Hope was something else.

She was gentle and simple, apparently satisfied to be able to look after her uncle while expecting nothing in return. Once or twice she had looked at Halliday in the appraising way women often did, sizing him up as though wondering about the caliber of the man within.

Halliday wondered if she was more interested in him as an ally?

He stretched out with the sky as his blanket, the moon hidden from sight behind a boulder. His horse was back in a clump of brush, content to settle there for the night. In such a place, Halliday would ordinarily be content, but now he had things on his mind.

Five hundred dollars was a lot of money. With that much in his pocket, he could drift for months and could select the jobs he wanted, not that he needed. He might even go to Sonora again, where a woman who reminded him a great deal of Hope Clayton might still be waiting.

Halliday's mouth broke into a smile. He had long ago discovered that nothing stayed the same, that memories played tricks on a man that got him into a fever of anticipation that more often than not led to a big letdown.

No, he decided then, he would never visit Sonora again.

When a light breeze stirred the brush behind him, Halliday stiffened, his hand automatically going to his gun and his hip lifting to make room for a fast draw. His horse whickered, warning Halliday that he might no longer be alone. It could be a jackrabbit or some animal searching for food.

Or it could be a man creeping up on him ...

Halliday came soundlessly to his feet, his clothes hugging his body as his leg, thigh and chest muscles stiffened. He didn't risk taking a step—there was always the chance of him stepping on a dry twig and snapping it.

He stood there, frozen, his gun clear of leather, his ears keened, his eyes searching. Then the faint clip-clop of a horse came to him from the valley, a mundane sound with no threat implicit in it.

He relaxed. He stood in shadow as he watched the trail bathed in moonlight. A moment later, a horse came into view, then the rider, hatless, long hair flowing down over her slender, rounded shoulders.

Hope Clayton paused for a moment, her eyes searching … for him …?

When she stopped her horse only yards from where he stood, he saw worry rut her brow.

"Mr. Halliday?"

"Come on up," Halliday said softly.

She straightened, startled to find him so close. Then she gave the horse a light touch of her heels; and drew rein short of the boulder, looking unsettled and uncertain.

"What is it?" Halliday asked. "Is your uncle okay?"

He saw her push her hair back, the action making her blouse tighten over her breasts.

"Yes, he's sleeping. He'll sleep till morning."

The words hung in the air between them, and Halliday wondered if he should read the meaning he wanted into them.

Hope looked beyond him into the gloom, and said, quietly, "Despite what he said, Mr. Halliday, I don't believe Latimer or his men will come tonight. Not after what happened in town today. They'll surely know we'll be ready for them."

"They won't know I'll be with you though," Halliday reminded her. "So maybe they won't care if you're ready or not."

Hope swung down from the horse and Halliday moved forward to take the horse's reins. She was here and that meant something to him. He decided to let her make the first move—if such a move was to come.

After he ground hitched her horse beside his own, he came back to the boulder to find her leaning against it, the moonlight reflecting on her lovely face. The soft light made her even more beautiful than he remembered, more desirable than ever.

"It's lovely up here," Hope said, looking at him with a tiny smile on her lips. "It's so quiet and peaceful, yet so lonely."

"Do you get lonely, ma'am?" Halliday asked.

"Often. I have only my uncle for company. Although I love him dearly and would never leave him, there's always something ... well, lacking."

"Lacking?" Halliday pressed.

"Yes. I don't really know how to explain it. I haven't been to many places nor have I met many people. I hardly know what life is all about, except what I've heard from some of my uncle's friends." She smiled shyly and looked down at her hands. "But I don't believe everything they tell me. Surely some of it is exaggerated?"

"Maybe if you told me what you mean, I could put my slant on it," Halliday said, watching the color rise in her cheeks and her body quiver with emotions she professed to know little about.

Then she was looking straight at him. There was confusion in her eyes, yet her hot gaze made such a demand on him that he couldn't ignore it. He rested his hand on her shoulder and fingered her hair lightly about her neck. The long, black hair was like silk, and from her smooth skin came the scent of pine and the river and the clear sky and all the things he liked most in life.

He felt her body stiffen under his touch. When he took his hand away, waiting for her to make the next move, she leaned against the boulder again, moonlight gleaming on her moist lips as they parted. Slowly, she came toward him. When their bodies touched, she went rigid again. Halliday still held back.

Then she looked up at him, her lips close to his now. Halliday put his hand on the back of her neck and drew her lips toward his. For a moment her kiss was unresponsive, then she stepped close so that her breasts pressed hard against his chest. He felt her breathing become more rapid and then suddenly she pushed him away and turned her back to him.

Halliday regarded her calmly. There was deep-rooted fear within her, he knew, but he wondered whether it was fear for what might happen between them, or fear for Latimer's gunnies.

"I'm so afraid," she whispered, turning back to face him.

"Maybe it's just the night," he said. "It is quiet up here."

"No, it's not that." Tears welled in her eyes. Her face was still flushed and she kept looking at him, her body trembling. "I don't know what it is. I've never felt like this before."

"Why did you come up here, Hope? Do you need a little excitement in your life?"

Hope straightened, her eyes suddenly going cold. "You know that's not it. I came up here … because … because …"

Her voice trailed off and she turned her back on him again.

Halliday let her lean against the boulder for some time before he took hold of her shoulders and turned her around. His hand brushed her breast as he reached for her chin. She sucked in a deep breath. He tilted her head back and she let him kiss her again, but then she struggled to move away. Suddenly, she jerked her head to the side and said;

"No! Please, no!"

Halliday looked straight into her eyes. He saw desire, want and need—but also fear. He let go of her.

She stood there, white-faced, shaken, unmoving. There was puzzlement in her eyes as she kept shaking her head. But she made no attempt to run to his horse.

"You'd better go back to your uncle," Halliday said. "If he wakes he'll be worried about you."

Hope nodded. When she finally did make a move, it was slowly, hesitantly, and she kept looking at him with no fear now but with a kind of wonder. Halliday turned his back on her and listened to her quick footsteps fade. He heard the creak of saddle leather and then the slap of reins down the horse's shoulders. He watched her go and felt the tension leave his body.

What did she hope to discover up here?

He was a man who so far had never forced himself on any woman. But he knew it might happen to her one day—it had to, for she was beautiful and lonely. Maybe some coarse-mouthed lowlife in some isolated hellhole would give her the love and tenderness she would remember for the rest of her life …

Forcing all thoughts of her from his mind, Halliday settled down again.

How long had she been up here? Five minutes … ten at the most? Time enough to leave him with visions flashing through his mind which he didn't really need at a time like this.

He took the stopper from his canteen and took a drink. The water was cool. He tipped some of it over his head and let it run down his face.

Then he thought again of Sonora …

It was just before dawn, and a deep, somber hush hung over the pass. Buck Halliday opened his eyes and his first thought was about Hope Clayton. It angered him. He rose, stretched his limbs and for nothing better to do, he swung into the saddle and rode down the pass.

The country ahead of him was flat, wide and empty. All about were the sounds of a new day stirring. He brought his mind back to what he had taken on, or rather, what he had decided not to take on. To hell with Hope and her conflicting emotions. He'd be better off on his own, heading where he liked.

He rode back through the pass and entered the valley. It had lost none of the previous night's charm. The timber was tall on the slopes, good for constructing whatever a man needed to put his roots down here. The grass was tall and as green as he had ever seen it.

Moving down the clearing, he noticed a thin wisp of smoke coming from the stone chimney. It looked like Hope was already up and about. Halliday hitched his horse, washed up in the trough beside the house, then he checked the water from the pump and found it good to the taste. He filled his canteen, hooked it back on the saddle horn and headed for the door.

The door was open, but he knocked anyway. When he got no answer, he called out Hope's name. When there was still no answer, he poked his head around the door and saw that the cabin was empty. The fire in the stove had almost burned itself out, and there was no sign that anybody had been preparing breakfast. Halliday walked inside, an uncomfortable feeling stirring inside him. That same feeling had been with him through the night, but he hadn't been able to come to grips with it. He moved about the room and stopped when he noticed that the old man's bunk had been stripped. Looking closely now at the things in the room, he saw that many of the little knick-knacks that had given the house its homely feeling were missing. The pile of ashes in the stove grating told him that the fire had been built to last.

Smothering a curse, Halliday hurried outside. He checked around the house and saw that the rig and the horse were gone. He stood there a moment, face set deep in thought.

Always a light sleeper, he couldn't understand how he had failed to hear the grind of wheels during the night or early this morning. Yet the rig was gone and he hadn't heard a sound. Surely, he thought, the old man had not gone to the trouble of padding the wheels and greasing the axles. But then, how else could they have left without him hearing them?

Suddenly, Halliday froze. He remembered Hope's visit in its entirety now, her uncertainty and worry, the way she'd allowed herself a certain amount of intimacy.

Halliday knew the answer as soon as the question formed in his head.

He walked back to the sorrel and was swinging into the saddle when he saw riders bearing down on him from the pass. Six-guns thundered and bullets began to fill the air about his ears.

Halliday jumped from the saddle, swung the sorrel behind him and drew his gun. The riders came down in a wide-spaced line. He knew he had to select his target carefully and make every bullet count.

Time had never been less on his side. He aimed, his gun bucked, and one rider rose in the saddle, swayed for a moment and then toppled to the ground and lay still.

Halliday swung his gun to cover the next target, but a bullet burned a crease along his forearm, making blood spurt. Cursing, he backed away, firing at will now, spacing his shots. His horse was tugging at its reins, so he finally grabbed it on a close rein and forced it into the cabin. Closing the door, he let the reins go, then broke a window with the butt of his gun.

Outside, six riders had formed a bunch and were hastily discussing their next move. Halliday recognized Zac Whelan and Rees Mann. The tall gunfighter looked as cool as he had in town and about as interested in this gunfight as he had been in the ruckus in the street. He stayed well out of range and was clearly giving the orders. When the five spread, Halliday held his fire. The advantage at this point was with him, so he bided his time as his horse stomped about behind him.

Then two riders came into six-gun range.

Halliday fired four rounds and both riders went down. The others veered away, then galloped back to Rees Mann.

"Three down," Halliday said to nobody in particular as he quickly reloaded, and was amused by the way Mann remonstrated with the men. Then he suddenly shouldered his horse through the others and slapped it into a run. He came straight at the cabin, lying low along the neck of the horse.

Halliday waited as the gunfighter approached, and did some more wondering. It now appeared to him as if the sneaky old-timer had sent Hope to him to keep him occupied, while he got the rig ready to be driven to a place where it wouldn't be detected.

With her job complete, Hope had then returned to the cabin. He had no doubt that she had left with the old man. They had made a fire big enough to last through the night, knowing he would not leave his post. They had also known that Latimer and his bunch would arrive that morning.

They had left him to fight their battle for them while they had driven the rig into the safety of the desert.

If he ever got his hands on that old jasper, he'd …

Halliday took a firm hold on his gun butt as Mann's bullets thudded into the cabin's walls. The gunfighter had run out of patience. Halliday considered this was all to his benefit. He ducked under the window sill and when the pounding of hoofs began to die away, he straightened.

Mann was about fifty feet away and was wheeling his horse around. They caught sight of each other through the gray light of dawn and both fired at precisely the same time.

Halliday felt a sharp sting of pain on the side of his head, but that was all and he knew it was just a graze. His own bullet nicked Mann's wrist, causing him to grip his gun in his left hand. When Mann fired again and his bullets whistled through the window, Halliday had a better idea of the gunfighter's ability.

He hammered out more shots as the other three, led by Zac Whelan, came charging at the cabin again. For the next few minutes, it seemed to Halliday that the cabin couldn't possibly withstand the relentless pounding of lead. The walls shook and dust sifted down from the rafters, threatening to choke him. He backed away from the window and then noticed another door leading into what could only be the back yard. He opened the door and saw fruit trees that had been planted in two neat rows.

With the cabin still shaking from the incessant pounding of bullets, Halliday led the horse through the doorway and swung into the saddle. If this was to be showdown day, he wanted his life to end outdoors. But as he turned the sorrel around, looking for a safe way up the slope, he noticed a wall of brush directly in front of him that didn't look as if nature had put it there. The sides and top were too even and its color clashed with the rest of the greenery in the yard.

He walked the horse toward the brush, and standing in the stirrups, looked over it to see a thin trail leading between the shoulders of two small hills. Halliday breathed a sigh of relief and sent the horse smashing through the brush. Beyond, he noticed the wheel tracks of the rig.

He settled the horse into an even lope and put the cabin and the Latimer bunch behind him.

He had just reached the top of a slope and saw the long sun-scorched stretch of desert ahead of him when the pounding of hoof beats told him that Mann, Whelan and the other two had discovered his means of escape.

Halliday looked about him, trapped on this high ground.

But Dick Clayton and his niece had come this way, so there had to be a way out. However, now wasn't the time to be looking for it. He worked his horse behind a boulder and from there went into a hollow. The branch of a tree felled by lightning hung as cover across the hollow's opening. Halliday sat saddle, knees locked about the horse's ribs to keep it steady. His gun fully loaded again, he was ready to make a stand.

Rees Mann came into view first, his jaw set tight. Halliday saw that he had bandaged his wrist with his bandana, which was scarlet with blood. It gave Halliday a measure of satisfaction to know that he had inflicted pain on the supposedly indestructible gunfighter. Next came Zac Whelan, his nervous eyes darting this way and that. Then came the other two, big men, their faces masks of dust from hard riding, and their clothes brush-torn. Their guns wavered in their hands, showing Halliday they were as nervous as Whelan.

Halliday remained still, the leaves of the tree branch making a speckled camouflage across his body.

Mann's gaze flicked his way, probed the rim of the hollow and then moved on. The gunfighter worked his horse about and was speaking when Whelan suddenly pointed to a gap in the brush on the far side. Mann rode toward the gap. From the saddle he kicked a dry heap of brush aside and nodded. But he held his horse there as if unwilling to lead the way. He waved Whelan ahead of him, and when the big ramrod had gone through the narrow opening, the other two gun hands followed. Mann still hesitated, his bleak eyes peering intently around.

"Halliday, if you're here, if you can hear me, then hear me good. Get out of this territory. I'll only tell you once."

With that, Mann went from sight.

Halliday didn't move for a full five minutes. He sat there, completely motionless, letting flies annoy his face and neck. When the silence remained unbroken, he came out of the saddle, hitched his horse and walked out of the hollow.

The sun shone hot now. He waved away the worrisome flies and crossed to where Mann and his cronies had gone from sight. He saw wheel tracks that the hoofs of their horses had not obliterated. Then further on, he saw the hoofmarks working along a path that was rutted by the tracks of a rig.

Uncle Dick's a smart old jasper, Halliday thought, as he returned to his sorrel. After checking his arm and finding the wound had stopped bleeding, he went into the saddle and looked thoughtfully about him.

Old Dick and his niece had fooled him well and truly. They had left him to face Latimer's bunch while they had fled. That in itself was enough to make him want to trail the pair and have it out with them. Added to that, he wanted the five hundred dollars the old-timer had promised him.

Seeing that the rig's wheel marks headed north, which was the way Ted Lomar had told Halliday to go, he saw no reason why he shouldn't take the lawman's advice.

FOUR

LATIMER'S LAND

It was quiet in the early afternoon, and so hot that Buck Halliday had dismounted and was moving on foot, giving his sorrel a much-needed breather. The crossing of the desert had all but exhausted his water supply, so now he was looking to replenish.

He had often been in country similar to this, so he carefully checked every line of the terrain, looking for a telltale sign of a rock cluster or anything that might lead him to the head of a spring. He made wide two-mile circles in the rocky country beyond the desert and it was sundown before he stopped for a rest, his search having proved fruitless.

His lips dry and cracked, he rested with his back against a deadfall and again thought about his future. Hope Clayton's taunting behavior still irked him, but he decided that searching for her might well prove to be of no real value. And if Rees Mann and Zac Whelan caught up with the rig, then Dick Clayton would surely rue this day.

Then Hope would have to fend for herself with something more powerful than a whip …

The air cooled as evening set in. With it came the stirring sounds of night animals foraging about for food. Halliday removed his boots, checked the tie-rein on his sorrel and made his way up a rocky slope. He sat in the dark, motion-less, waiting, willing to wait out the night while his throat burned dry and craved for water.

Finally, he heard the rustle of some animal moving through the brush below him. Halliday waited until the sound died, then he worked his way on his belly onto a narrow trail. It took him twenty minutes to follow the trail down to a hollow where a jackrabbit sat on its haunches, its mouth working rapidly as it drank. Halliday waited for it to have its fill before he hurried forward and dropped onto his stomach.

He drank slowly, then, taking the canteen from his shoulder, he filled it, rose and with no reason for stealth any longer, strode back up the slope to his waiting sorrel. He watered the horse from his hat, tied the canteen to the saddle pommel and then stretched out and slept.

"Uncle?"

Hope Clayton regarded the craggy-featured old-timer over the rim of her fire-blackened coffee mug. Her uncle was repairing a rein and frowning with the concentration needed to do the job properly. His face reflected the strain of the day's hard driving, for he had taken over the reins late the previous night and hadn't stopped even to give the horse a break during the long, hot crossing.

"Yeah, girl?" Clayton said finally.

"Are you sure Mr. Halliday will be all right?"

"A man can't be sure of anythin' in this world, darlin'," he told her. "But I'm willin' to bet money that tomorrow is gonna be as hot as today and we're gonna need every bit of strength we've got to make it to Parson Falls. You'd best stretch out now and get all the sleep you can. I'll keep watch and wake you in time to pack."

Hope sipped her coffee and looked frowningly down into the cup. After a moment, she said, "I certainly hope he will be all right. After all, he did help us in town and he was willing to keep watch for us during the night. I think we did wrong sneaking off like we did."

The old man looked up sharply at her. "He happened into our lives when we most needed him, girl, which, the way I look at it, was too bad for him. I figgered it out right … it was him or us. And with you to look after, I didn't spend long figurin' on which way it was gonna be. Now forget about him. He's a big man and he sure enough knows how to look after hisself. If he makes it, I guess he'll be sour at us, and with some right. But what the hell? We're in the clear and in another two days, we should link up with the stage trail into Parson Falls. We might even run into that representative the railroad was dyin' to meet us. If we do, we'll sign, get our money and head straight for California."

Hope bit at her lower lip and stared at him. "Uncle Dick, I'm not that interested in the money."

"You ain't, eh? All right, tell me how money ain't important. Money is what puts clothes on a man's back, a horse beneath him, and food in his belly. It does a hell of a lot fer a woman, too, maybe even more, with all the finery and frippery a woman likes to buy. Now see here, girl, all day long you been moonin' alongside me. You ain't spoke but a couple decent words to me in all that time and all I'm doin' is savin' your skin from a bunch of gunnies. I'm tellin' you for the last time, forget that feller. He's been on the drift for most of his life. He knows the score."

Hope put her cup down and looked past her uncle to the wall of rock that curved around them. She sensed that her uncle had selected this place because of his fear of a night attack. Yet she could not believe that the country they had traveled that day could possibly be covered by anybody else following them. It had been the hottest day she'd ever experienced and she longed to wash her body of the dust and sweat.

"Will you pay Mr. Halliday if we meet him again, Uncle?" Hope asked a moment later.

That earned her a deeper scowl.

"Halliday, Halliday, Halliday! You gonna keep right on talkin' about him, ain't ya? He do somethin' to you last night I should know about and which you're keepin' to yourself? By hell, if he so much as—"

"He did nothing to me," Hope answered angrily. "He could have done anything in the world to me up there but he didn't. And God knows I wanted him to. So if I find out that he

71

died trying to help us, I'm going to regret it for the rest of my life!"

Clayton tossed the mended reins aside and hopped to his feet. He crossed to Hope on a tree branch he was using as a crutch. "What's this you're sayin', girl? You regret not lettin' that drifter bed you down? What's come over you? I've tried to bring you up right, just like your ma and pa would have wanted me to. You gonna throw all them years I gave you back in my face and tell me I done wrong by my dead brother and his poor wife?"

Hope struggled with her emotions and stood there tall and graceful, knowing the picture of loveliness she presented.

"I'm no longer a girl," she said. "So I don't want you to call me that again. I'm a woman and for a long time now I've been thinking about getting myself a man. I don't think that's anything but natural. I want a man and if that man happens to be Buck Halliday, then I will be anything but disappointed. In fact, I'll give myself to him gladly … with no strings attached."

The old man stepped back as if she had struck him. He pulled on his gray straggle of a beard and shook his head in disbelief. "Am I hearin' right?"

"Yes, Uncle, you're hearing right. There are a few other things you should know, too, and one of them is the fact that you never discuss anything with me. You never give me the chance to voice my opinions. It's always what you do or are going to do. My opinion means nothing. It's as though I don't matter to you at all."

"You matter, girl, by hell—you matter more to me than anythin' alive. But I'm tellin' you now that I know what's best fer you and fer me, and as long as I can sink my teeth into a cud, why then, girl—"

"I'm *not* a girl, Uncle. This is the last time I'll remind you of the fact. As for knowing what's best for me, I might have wanted to stay in the valley and work the ranch. I loved that place. It was so quiet and green, and so peaceful. If it was worked right it would support both of us and give us all the comfort we need."

"Worked right?" Clayton barked. "You tellin' me that I— ?"

"Uncle Dick, I'm telling you that you're anything but a hard worker. The opportunity to sell the place and get out suited you just fine. Your desire for money stopped you from accepting Latimer's offer of a trade for another place. Only a mind as cunning as yours where money is concerned could possibly have suspected some ulterior motive on Mr. Latimer's part. Of course, you were right about him, but in admitting that I'm forced to admit a few other things to myself. You are greedy, sneaky, grasping ... and you're a liar."

Clayton gaped at her and stepped back another pace, scrubbing a hand across his neck.

"Now see here, girl ... young woman. I ain't about to take that from you or anybody else. I always done what I figgered was best for the two of us and I aim to keep right on makin' the decisions. So you shut down and don't argue with an old man who don't have nobody left in the whole world but you."

But Hope would not be mollified. "Uncle Dick, from now on, we will not desert friends or put anybody in a position where he might get hurt, regardless of what rewards we might be able to get from his misfortune. I don't think we can ever do anything to rectify what we did last night. I can only hope and pray that Mr. Halliday escaped from Latimer's killers. And if we succeed in this, then we'll put aside some money to make sure he gets paid for helping us."

Clayton tugged at his lower lip and scowled. But this time he remained quiet, remembering other times in his life when he had done verbal battle with a woman just like her. By hell, he told himself, Hope was the image of her mother, who put his brother in his grave long before his time.

Clayton turned and crossed to the rig. He put his crutch up against the wheel and took down his old rifle, felt a twinge of pain from his bandaged ankle and limped back past Hope to sit on a smooth-topped boulder from where he could see down into the desert.

The nerve of her, he thought ... and the spunk, too.

Why did women have to speak their minds so openly?

Ten minutes alone with a damned drifter and he'd turned her head to mush. He decided that when they reached California, he'd invest in a decent, profitable town business, and then he'd watch her carefully. Given the slightest chance, she might become what her mother had been and hand all menfolk within her range one big taste of hell.

On her part, Hope spread out a blanket, and with her conscience somewhat cleared, she settled down and looked up at the stars. She raised a hand to her breasts and thought of Buck Halliday. His touch had sent a thrill up her spine.

If he was with her now, she knew she wouldn't be able to resist him … she wouldn't want to.

Rees Mann stood perfectly still. The sound of Zac Whelan using his authority to get the other men to unsaddle the horses annoyed him. He had come to dislike Whelan a great deal. The man had proved himself to be a bully and something of a coward. He was also dim-witted. If it hadn't been for the man's foolish ways, he wouldn't have had to ride from Cannon Creek with a lawman eyeing him off and a drifter defiantly opposing him.

Mann smoothed his hands down his pants leg. His wrist still hurt, but it was his pride that had suffered the most pain. Buck Halliday had shot him. It had been five years since any man had been able to do that, and even then, it had taken four men and an ambush to achieve it. The four had died under Mann's blazing guns. But Buck Halliday was still alive.

The door of the little cabin opened and a short, fat man stepped outside. His face was round and bloated. The dark, evil smelling smoke from his cigar all but screened his piggy eyes.

"Well?" he asked. "You get 'em?"

"No," Mann said.

Whelan had come up behind Mann and he remained in the background as if wanting no part of this confrontation between the gunfighter and the fat man with the cigar. The others stood back, shoulder to shoulder, uneasy in the sundown shadows.

The fat man raised his head and his dark gaze swept past Mann to take in Whelan first and then the other two.

"Where's Collinson, Barker and Jones?" Whelan asked.

"Dead," Mann told him.

The cigar rolled across the fat man's fat lips. "Dead? Three of 'em? What the hell did you run into? A troop of cavalry?"

"A drifter named Halliday," Mann said. "A good man with a gun, a man who moves fast, makes no mistakes, and who doesn't give a damn if you keep trailin' him to the end of the earth."

The fat man worked his neck and pulled the cigar free of his thick lips. He studied the sloppy end of the weed, gave a grunt and hurled the cigar aside. The fat man eyed Mann more intently, shaking his head a little, then sighing.

"Well, Rees, I guess you'd best step inside and tell me all about it. I reckon I know enough about you to realize you walked into something you weren't expectin', otherwise this drifter would be dead—wouldn't he?"

"He would be and he will be," was Mann's clipped reply. He brushed past the fat man who turned to Whelan and said;

"Keep them horses quiet. Get a fire goin'. No smoke. Then stick close to this place in case I need you in a hurry."

Whelan was about to speak when the fat man turned his back on him. When the door closed, Whelan wiped his oily face with a soiled bandanna. Suddenly, he whirled on the others and growled;

"Well, you heard Mr. Latimer! Get a fire goin'. And get some coffee and grub together. I'm starved near outta my mind."

The two men hurried off without argument and Whelan sat on a tree stump and his stubby fingers patted the sore spots on his face. There were many of them. He grumbled to himself and looked into the distance, remembering how close he had come to being killed. Halliday hadn't wasted lead in getting Collinson, Barker and Jones, and Whelan considered it was just plain good luck that he hadn't collected the bullet that had shattered Mann's wrist. So he sat there and first he wished to hell that Halliday had gone the other way, and then that he was down in Pecos country where somebody else would have to worry about him. Whelan didn't mind fighting old Dick Clayton and his niece, but he wanted absolutely nothing to do with the drifter named Buck Halliday!

Inside the cabin, Aldo Latimer poured two drinks and handed a glass across the table to Mann. He then cut the end off a cigar with a pocketknife and pushed the weed between his lips. He rolled the cigar in his mouth for a time before he said;

"Tell me about it, Rees. Hell, this ain't how we planned it, is it?"

"Far from it," Mann said. "You know about the Cannon Creek ruckus?"

"Only what you told me last night, which wasn't much. But I saw the bruises and the cuts on the men. That Halliday's doing?"

"Him and the Bar-Nine bunch. No matter. After we left you last night, we cut back to the Clayton valley and went through the gap. There we ran into Halliday. He had the cover, used it well—got three of the boys before I went in after him. He ran, but we didn't know he'd gone till we burned down the cabin and he didn't come out. Later, we found a trail back of the cabin, one nobody knew about."

"Back of the cabin?" Latimer said. "Hell, I didn't even know about that. I figured that cabin was vulnerable to attack from the front, and once cornered in that valley, Clayton would have no chance."

"You underestimated him, just as I underestimated Halliday," Mann said sourly. "So we're even on that score. As for the rest of it, we trailed Halliday, lost him, then continued until we picked up Clayton's trail. I figure they're about six, seven hours ahead of us, but stuck with one horse and a heavy rig to pull. Another day of traveling in that country and Clayton will slow to a walk. Then we'll have him."

Despite Mann's show of confidence, Latimer was still a worried man.

"That'll give him a whole day on us, Rees. He can cover a lot of territory in that time."

"It'll get him only half of the way to Parson Falls," Mann said. He leaned back and waved cigar smoke from his face. "We'll rest for the night, take along a change of horses and keep after him till we pin him down."

Latimer nodded, indicating that the plan suited him. But then his brow rutted again. "What about Halliday?"

"I don't rightly know about him," Mann admitted. "He might keep tagging us or he might figure he's had too many close shaves so far. If he comes, I'll handle him."

Latimer stood up, finished his drink and opened the door of the cabin. As the fresh air burst through the opening and he saw his three hired guns settled down near a smokeless fire, he said;

"Well, we're short-handed, I guess, but the loss cuts down the payment we have to make to those rannies, Rees. The girl and the old man shouldn't cause us much trouble in the open, eh?"

"Very little," Mann agreed.

Mann got to his feet and joined Latimer in the doorway. He studied the fat man's profile for a moment, then he turned away from the cigar's black smoke. There were lots of things about Aldo Latimer that he didn't like. But he conceded that Latimer was a thinker and not a complainer. All in all, the fat man was good enough company for the time being, but just as soon as he got his stake, Mann meant to cut out on his own. He didn't like working as part of a group. He had worked for too long on his own to change his ways now. Men who'd hunted him had either lost his trail or were buried in lonely graves.

He was a loner and didn't care. A long time ago fate had ruled that he earn a reputation with his guns. When one killing led to another then another, he saw life as an expendable thing. But he didn't hate. Nor did he love. He just went his way, asking for nothing and receiving very little in return.

Now, walking from Latimer, he ignored a call for coffee from Whelan and strolled into the shadows of evening.

Whelan waited for Mann to get out of earshot, then he turned to Latimer and said, "Did he tell you everything?"

"He told me Halliday beat the stuffin' outta you."

Whelan frowned up at him. "I wouldn't say it like that, Mr. Latimer. Hell, we were jumped by that drifter and—"

"Sure, Zac. But hear me now. If you can't handle men, don't get the idea you can take your bitterness out on a woman. When we catch up with Hope Clayton and her uncle, you concentrate on the old man. I want you to leave the girl to me. You hear?"

Whelan licked his lips and wiped his mouth on a sleeve. In the firelight, his face was ugly. "I ain't ever had no intention of—"

"Keep that in mind, Zac. That woman is mine. Soon as you've finished supper, turn in—and no drinking. We've got a long ride ahead and I want you fit and healthy."

Latimer went to where the horses were tethered. He ran a hand gently over the nose of his horse and spoke soothingly to it. But all the time his mind was thinking of Hope Clayton. He couldn't wait to get his hands on her. From the first moment he saw her, he couldn't stop thinking about her. He had never wanted a woman so badly. He didn't completely understand his feelings himself, but he knew that until he had her in his arms, the craving for her would not go away. He settled down, drew on his cigar and thought about his bunch. It had started out as seven … now it was down to four. And all in the space of one day.

But surely five were enough to bring an old man and a girl down to size and get a paper signed. After that he'd get rid of Clayton and cut out with the girl. But what would he do about Rees Mann? Having Mann about worried him. There was something about the man that reminded Latimer of a lobo wolf.

What if Mann wanted to tag along with him to the border? What if, in Mann's coldhearted soul, there was a desire for Hope Clayton, too?

Latimer could see only trouble ahead if that were the case. He was honest enough to split the money, but sharing a woman had little appeal. Still, he told himself, maybe he was trying to cross a river before he came to it. Maybe the river would run smooth and slow and the crossing would pose no threat. He certainly hoped so, because if it proved to be otherwise … well, he'd just have to kill Rees Mann.

FIVE

JUST PLAIN DRIFTING

Buck Halliday awoke with his decision made. For the last few minutes, he'd been watching a lizard creeping warily in the shadow of a deadfall log. The pulsing heart of the lizard made its whole body quiver. The creature stopped and didn't move. It was biding its time. Halliday couldn't see its prey, but he felt sure it would be a thing of beauty. To him it seemed that beauty was always being hunted.

He rolled up his blanket and remembered how beautiful Hope Clayton had appeared in the soft light of the pass.

Was he like the lizard, biding his time until he could claim his beautiful prey?

He smiled and brushed a hand through his hair before he picked up his hat. He raked up the coals of last night's fire with his boot and fanned the coals into flame with his hat. He added sticks of dead wood and set the coffeepot on a rock. Sitting there with the cool air of morning washing over him, he felt relaxed, knowing there were thousands of trails he could follow to their end. He didn't really care which trail he took or what the future held for him, because inside him was a spirit that never allowed him to stay in one place too long.

After drinking three mugs of coffee, he was still reluctant to leave this peaceful place. His canteen was full, his sorrel was well rested. He sat back and watched the lizard strike, its beak open to receive its first mouthful of the day. He picked up a rock and hurled it at the lizard, sending it scurrying away.

That done, he packed his bedroll behind the saddle and drop his washed coffeepot and mug into the saddlebag. He swung up and the sorrel moved off, instinctively taking the direction it had been following the previous day. Halliday grinned. The horse often did the choosing for them and he saw no reason why he should deny him the choice on such a glorious morning.

He followed a brush trail down to the flat country and left the desert behind him. The day's silence was a somehow comforting thing, and he felt no loneliness. He rode slowly, not thinking about anything but what was around him. This was the life he craved—a man unharnessed and on the drift, with no one to complicate it.

He stopped on a rise thirty minutes later after seeing a cloud of dust behind a small hill. The dust seemed to cling to the brush growing out of the rocky walls. His stare thinned as he sat there motionless, waiting for the dust to settle.

Ten minutes of waiting told him that somebody had passed that way. He checked his gun and heeled the sorrel on. Down here in the flat country, he had room to move, and plenty of cover if necessity arose.

Likely Rees Mann, Zac Whelan and their two buddies had come this way, he decided. Perhaps, like himself, they had rested for the night after the hard desert crossing. But he didn't think the shrewd old Uncle Dick would hang about while he could put more distance between himself and his pursuer.

Aldo Latimer.

Halliday had not met the man as yet and wondered what manner of man he was. And what motives apart from greed made him order his men to attack and kill an old man and a defenseless young woman. Evidently, he was so sure of himself he felt he could tell the law to go take a powder.

Now well into the flat country, Halliday put the sorrel into an easy lope and warned himself not be caught napping.

The five men sat their horses and looked at the distant figure riding toward them.

"It's Halliday," Rees Mann said to Aldo Latimer.

Latimer scowled. "Damn him! You think he mebbe works for Clayton?"

Mann shrugged. "I don't know." He turned and beckoned for Zac Whelan to ride alongside. When the big, burly-chested cowhand was beside them, Mann asked;

"You ever see Halliday in Clayton's company durin' the last week or so?"

Whelan thought for a moment, then frowned. "Nope, can't say as how I did, Rees."

"Go check with the others."

Whelan rode away and returned minutes later, shaking his head.

"None of us ever saw Halliday before he bought into that ruckus in the street. He ain't ever been seen before with Shelvy and his scurvy crowd, neither. I reckon he's just a damned interferin' troublemak—"

"What you reckon doesn't interest me in the least," Mann cut him short, and turned to Latimer. "Could be that what you figure might be right, Aldo—that our friend had merely stopped over in Cannon Creek lookin' for work. Then when Whelan started to pester that old buzzard in the street, he decided to maybe get himself a quick reputation which might help him find some work. Whatever it was, he doesn't seem to have found any. Maybe he just rode out and that's how he linked up with the Claytons. How or why doesn't really matter, does it? Maybe the girl appealed to him or maybe he just saw a chance to get a free feed. Maybe the old man even promised to pay him. Who knows what goes on in that old buzzard's head? Turnin' our first offer down has sure got me thinkin' though."

Mann wiped a hand across his brow and a thin smile stretched across his mouth. He stared down into the flat country they had left an hour ago and let his gaze travel the ridge line they planned to cross next.

"Whatever made Halliday stay on at the Clayton place, it's got him on the wrong side of us. Not to mention killing three of our men."

Latimer grunted something under his breath and glared back along the trail. He saw again the lone rider coming through the sagebrush.

The fact that the man was riding easily and clearly taking his time, had him confused.

"He doesn't look like he's trailin' us," Latimer opined.

Mann nodded. "He doesn't look like he's doing that at all. But it's Buck Halliday, Aldo, and we're gonna settle with him right now."

Latimer looked ahead. "We don't have much time," he reminded Mann. "Clayton and the girl will be goin' as hard as they can and maybe that horse of theirs is sturdy enough to keep up the pace."

"We've got mebbe a half-hour to wait," Mann said, and pointed ahead. "These two trails meet at a point over there, where the boulders rise up on that slope. It's a good place for an ambush." Mann signaled to Whelan and pointed out the place. "Take the others and get beyond that last rocky point. Leave your horses and hide your-selves in the rocks. Aldo and I will take positions down lower, one on either side of the trail. When I give the signal, I want all guns blazing."

Whelan nodded. "Don't worry. We'll get him."

"Hold it, Zac. First I want you to see how much Halliday is mixed up in all this."

Latimer was frowning heavily again, and Whelan looked uncomfortable. But when Mann's hard stare settled on him, Whelan nodded and rode off. Latimer drew his horse beside Mann's, and said;

"I don't go for these theatrics, Rees. Hell, there are five of us. Why not just ride down there and put an end to him?"

Mann smiled coldly. "Because he's already proved he's more than a capable man with a gun. And too damned capable not to get one or two of us before we could finish him off."

"You sound like you almost admire the man, Rees," Latimer said. "Hell, he's nothin' but a—"

"Top man with a gun, Aldo, make no mistake about that. Too damned good for my likin'. As for admirin' him, mebbe I do—but that only means I'm more determined to kill him. I don't like the idea of a man like him doggin' my trail."

Mann motioned for Latimer to take up his position on the opposite side of the trail. He waited in the shade, keeping his horse in check and watching the lone rider take the rise. Mann brought out his gun and hooked a leg over his saddle horn. He was smiling broadly, plainly enjoying himself …

Buck Halliday rode warily, remembering the screen of dust and looking for more of it. But the country seemed empty now, too rocky to hold hoofmarks or to throw up anymore dust. Still, he kept his ears pricked for any alien sound and he watched his sorrel's head for the slightest warning that they might have company.

He was about to enter a pass between two short, slightly sloped hills when shooting broke out ahead. He looked up the trail and saw where a track leading to high ground, evidently to cross the hills at that point and save considerable ground for anybody traveling between Cannon Creek and Parson Falls.

As the shooting continued, his mind was busy trying to read it. It was plain there was more than one gun. Perhaps three or four. But he couldn't pick out the boom of a rifle in the noise. And Dick Clayton had an old rifle which he would surely be using if he was under attack.

Halliday drew rein, suspicion nagging at his mind.

Was it a trick?

He had ridden across open country and would surely have been seen by Mann and his cronies if they were still traveling this same route. They wouldn't be too far ahead if they'd stopped to camp for the night after the hard desert crossing. He scrubbed a hand across his neck, relieving some of the tension beginning to form there, then he drew his gun, turned his sorrel off the trail and headed for a stand of timber to the southwest.

Gaps in the trees showed where many pine trees had been felled. If this was good enough country to encourage settlers to put down roots, perhaps he would find a place to make camp.

He had gone only a hundred yards when he sighted a group of riders bearing down on the boulder cluster from the highest ridge point. Even from this distance, Halliday recognized the boyish figure of Tim Shelvy, hat bouncing on the back of his neck, gun blasting away with an exuberance that was more noise than effect.

Halliday wheeled his sorrel to a halt. The gunfire behind the boulders suddenly ceased, then broke out louder a short time later. He kicked his horse into a run. If this had been a trap, Shelvy and his outfit had left the door open so he could get through it.

He belted his horse into a run as bullets ricocheted off boulders around him and whined away. Dust rose high as Shelvy's riders tore down the slope, loosening rubble and kicking up brush.

Halliday saw one of Shelvy's crew topple from the saddle, then a second veered off toward the timber, clutching his chest. But Tim Shelvy, still firing wildly, swung past the biggest of the boulders and went into the gateway of the trail.

Halliday kicked his horse into a harder run and went through only a minute behind him. He swung away from the dense cloud of dust and broke into clean air against the wall of a huge boulder. A bullet tugged at his hide jacket and made him pull his sorrel about. Then he spotted the short-bodied fat man with a cigar stuck between his teeth who was punching off bullets at him.

Halliday's gun spat flame, and two bullets thudded into Aldo Latimer. The fat man let out a piercing scream, toppled off the flat surface of a rock and broke his neck when he hit the ground.

Halliday swung out of the saddle as higher up the trail, Tim Shelvy stood with his feet planted wide, emptying his gun at two hard-riding gun hands.

Halliday saw one of the men go down. Then the man in black, still carrying the bloodied bandanna on his wrist, broke out of the dust cloud and stormed past him.

Halliday ducked as bullet after bullet hammered into the boulder beside him. So fast had Rees Mann come at him that he had time to get off only one shot before the man in black was gone.

Halliday held his rearing horse hard until it quietened, then he pushed it between two large boulders. Gun refilled, he rode back out into the action.

Tim Shelvy was down on one knee now, nursing a bloodied left shoulder but still punching off shots. Zac Whelan was backing away from him, firing blindly, clearly not wasting any time taking aim, just trying to fight his way to safety.

Three Bar-Nine cowhands converged on another gun hand scrambling up the trail on his hands and knees. Bullets ripped into him, hurled his body about like a rag doll and sent him tumbling back down the slope. He hit a shoulder of rock, bounced, rolled to the left, then fell headlong to stony ground and did not move.

Now only Zac Whelan remained unharmed. White-faced and sweating, he was almost to the edge of the timbered slope and his last chance for freedom. He emptied his gun, then turned and fled.

Halliday reached Shelvy's side and saw the young cowhand lift his gun, clench his teeth and take aim.

"I'd like to take him alive," Halliday said.

"To hell with that. We've been waitin' for a chance like this to square accounts with that bastard. But every time we saw him, he had his bunch with him. Now he's on his own and so help me, he's gonna get it."

"I want him to talk first," Halliday said, grim-faced.

Shelvy swore at him but Halliday pushed him aside, then he waved for the other men to stop firing. When they did, he walked straight up the middle of the trail. Zac Whelan saw him coming with a glance over his shoulder and stopped, breathing heavily.

His gun raised, Halliday, said;

"Stay where you are, Whelan. Take one more step and it'll be your last."

Whelan looked fearfully about him, and saw the Shelvy crew lined up. He had only a couple of yards to go to reach the cover of the trees. But his feet felt like lead and refused to move. He still held his gun in front of his waist, but the barrel was pointed at the ground.

"It wasn't none of my doin', Halliday," he cried out. "You tell this crazy bunch that. I ain't killed nobody and I didn't want any part of this."

"You're a liar!" Tim Shelvy snarled.

When Halliday saw the cowhand take a firmer grip on his gun butt, he called out quickly;

"Drop the gun and put your hands in the air, Whelan! If you don't do it fast, one of us will cut you down."

Whelan switched his glance to Tim Shelvy. He couldn't help but see the hate and the lust to kill in the man's eyes. Sobbing in terror, he threw his gun away and raised his hands above his head. Then he took a hesitant step toward Halliday and stopped.

"Keep them away from me, Halliday. I'm givin' myself up to you, not to them crazies."

"Then keep comin' and you won't get hurt, mister," Halliday told him.

Gulping painfully and trying to keep the sweat from his eyes, Whelan walked slowly down the slope. But just as he drew up only a few paces from Halliday, Tim Shelvy leaped forward and clubbed his gun butt against the side of Whelan's head.

97

Shelvy went toward him again with the gun butt raised, but Halliday caught his hand and jerked him back.

"You can have what's left of him," Halliday said, then he grabbed Whelan by his shirtfront and slammed him against a giant-sized boulder.

He hit the blubbering and dazed Whelan three times with the back of his hand before he hurled him to the ground. Then he stood over him as, from a long way off, came the muffled tattoo of a galloping horse.

Rees Mann was making good his escape.

SIX

A STORY TOLD

Zac Whelan looked terrified as Tim Shelvy closed in on him. He could taste the blood in his mouth and could feel it running down both cheeks. He knew he was badly hurt and was terrified over the likelihood of suffering more pain. All he wanted was to save his hide and forget he had ever met Aldo Latimer and Rees Mann.

"Your bunch killed two of our friends," Shelvy said, "and we're holdin' you for it."

Shelvy prodded the outstretched Whelan in the ribs with his boot and then he took a length of rope from one of the crew. He stood over the sobbing Whelan and slowly fashioned a noose. Meantime, Halliday had organized the collection of the dead, among whom was the fat man he'd killed.

"Whelan can wait, Tim," Halliday said. "First we've got to get these men buried and see to the wounded. Then I want a few minutes with him. After that you can do what you like with him."

Shelvy nodded grimly as he tightened the noose. Looking into Whelan's eyes, he said;

"We'll give you plenty of time to think about what you did to my men and to that girl last year, mister."

Whelan shook his head despairingly. "I never done nothin' to you, Shelvy. You got it all wrong. Sure, I rode with Latimer, but hell, I was on his payroll. I worked cattle, did some chores and now and again I went to town and got drunk. But I never done nothin' to make you want to kill me, I swear it!"

Shelvy's boot crashed into Whelan's ribs again and then he said tonelessly, "Mister, Ben Stocker's back there, dead, with two bullets in him. Ben came here to pay you back for what you did to his daughter. Do you remember that night on the trail when she was coming home alone and you just happened to come across her?"

Whelan shook his head again and blood from his chin dripped to the ground. One of his front teeth was loose and blood ran from the corner of his mouth.

"She … she asked me, I swear it! Practically begged me! Hell, you all knew what she was like. I didn't do no more than plenty of others had done before me. Hell, some of your own boys have been with her. I saw it more'n once."

Shelvy kicked him again and looked about for a suitable tree. Finding one, he ordered a man to guard the prisoner while he got the rope ready.

It went over the limb on his first throw and he let the noose slide down to the right height and anchored the other end to the trunk. Satisfied, he tore his shirt and inspected his shoulder wound. All this time Halliday watched him carefully, ready to step in if he tried to go ahead with the hanging.

Then he saw Shelvy nod at him and Halliday turned to watch the bodies being carried in.

The two Shelvy hands were laid out under the shade of a nearby tree while the bloodied, unshaven cowhands were dropped by the trail in the sun, along with the fat man dressed in the expensive clothes. The man's soft leather boots would do justice to a Spanish dude, but one toe had been shot away and blood filled what remained of the boot.

"That's Latimer," Shelvy pointed out.

"The top man?" Halliday said.

"Yeah. He hired the gunnies and he brought Mann out here to keep an eye on his range."

"He owns land out here?"

Shelvy nodded. "A stretch of country back of these hills. Nobody seems to know how many head he runs. It's hardscrabble country that nobody wanted. But he did okay for himself at the cattle sales and he always seems to have plenty of money to throw around for free drinks. Rumor has it that his outfit rustles what he sells but nobody so far has been able to prove it. Sneaky and shrewd, if you ask me."

Halliday made himself a cigarette. Some of the Shelvy men had already started digging graves. Watching them, his mind traveled back to his trouble in town. Somehow he'd known it would come to this. Now that it had, he felt no relief. He should be able to relax, he told himself. So why couldn't he?

"What got your outfit and his at loggerheads, Tim?" Halliday asked.

Shelvy shrugged, "We were in town one day and the Latimer bunch rode in. We started drinkin' and some words were exchanged, to begin with, mainly just joshin'. Then a fight broke out and before you knew it, we damn near wrecked the Red Garter. After that, Lomar said we should drink only at the Lovely Lucy and the Latimer crowd was to drink at the Red Garter. That suited both of us, and for a time things were quiet. Then Ben's girl arrived home from town one day in one hell of a mess. Seems Whelan had his way with her. We got the boys together and paid Latimer a visit. There was gunplay and a couple our boys got wounded before we had to pull back. Ben used to ride off on his own looking for Whelan, and once when he entered Latimer land, he saw some of our beeves on Latimer's land. That sealed it for us, and for a long time now it's been our crowd and theirs takin' shots at each other every time our paths cross. Like in town the other day. Now it's come to this."

"The end," Halliday said.

Shelvy nodded. "Just about. All that's left is for us to bury our dead and string Whelan up."

"What about Rees Mann?" Halliday asked.

Shelvy studied him gravely. "I haven't forgotten him. But where the hell is he?"

"He cut and ran."

Shelvy's brows arched. "Are you sayin' he ran and left his friends for dead?"

"We exchanged shots, but in the confusion, he got away. Last I saw, he was ridin' hell for leather away."

"Then we'd best get after him. Latimer's dead, Whelan will be soon, and I don't reckon the rest of this outfit will be doin' anybody any harm again. Just wait till my boys are finished with the buryin'."

Shelvy went off and Halliday turned and studied Whelan again. The man's frightened gaze kept sweeping over the Shelvy men as if he was loath to miss any part of what they were doing. Finally, he caught Halliday's eye. Wiping his face with a bloodied sleeve, he said hoarsely;

"For hell's sake, help me, will you? We locked horns, sure, but I was the only one hurt. I don't want no more to do with this outfit or this range. I just want outta here."

"What you'd better do is tell me what Mann's up to."

Whelan worked cramp out of his shoulders. Finally, he pushed himself to his knees and knelt there with the morning sunlight streaming across his face.

"I'll trade my life for any information you want to know. Deal?"

"I can't speak for Tim Shelvy. After all, you killed two of his crew. So why don't you tell me what Mann's up to, and I'll see what I can do?"

Whelan blinked and shook his head. "Hell, I don't know a damn thing about him. It's always been him and Latimer, makin' up their minds without discussin' anythin' with me or anyone else."

"Were they partners then?"

"Kinda, I guess," Whelan said. "Latimer hired us to work the range. The usual cowhand stuff. Now and again he told us to round up some steers that didn't have his brand on 'em. We didn't ask questions, just did what we was paid to do. What else could we do? Hell, there must've been times when you've been made do things you didn't think was right, ain't that so?"

When Halliday didn't respond, Whelan wiped his face, wincing when his bandanna hit the raw flesh there.

"Maybe you mightn't have done things like that, Halliday, but then we ain't all like you. I'm admittin' it now to you that I ain't all that strong. I ain't mean and I certainly ain't a lowdown dog. If you don't get me outta here, they'll hang me for sure."

Halliday twisted up a smoke, and seeing Whelan's eyes on the paper cylinder, he tossed it to him. Whelan failed to catch it but scooped it from the ground, stuck it in his mouth and turned his face up to Halliday for a light. Halliday thumbed a match into life, and as he leaned forward, his gun came within Whelan's reach.

Halliday watched Whelan's gaze go down to the gun butt and saw his mouth twitch in some forlorn hope. But when Whelan made a move for the gun, Halliday brought his knee up under Whelan's jaw.

Whelan slumped back and shook his head.

"I wasn't gonna—"

"I know you weren't, but only because I wasn't going to let you. So keep talking … you've told me nothing yet."

Whelan shifted the crushed cigarette around in his bruised lips and accepted Halliday's light. Then he sat back on his haunches, his face draining of color as Shelvy approached them. "Finished with him, Buck?" Shelvy asked.

"Not yet. Bear with me awhile longer, Tim."

"Sure, sure," Shelvy was quick to answer. "The boys are finishin' their chores and they'll have the horses ready to move in five minutes."

He looked at the sweating Whelan and grinned. Whelan let the smoke fall from his mouth and didn't bother to pick it up.

"Why'd you have to go and burn down the Claytons' cabin?" Shelvy asked him.

Whelan shook his head in denial of the charge.

"It's just the sort of thing you'd do, Whelan, like poisonin' a man's drinkin' water. Or shootin' somebody in the back, maulin' a young girl, them kind of things. Mister, you got a stink about you that's gotta be buried so it don't stench up the whole territory."

Whelan's face quivered and his eyes widened in fear. His breathing stopped, then came back hard and fast, and he sat back on his haunches, looking like a man resigned to his fate.

Shelvy turned away and regarded Halliday thoughtfully. "We saw the smoke late yesterday, Buck. That's how we found the trail back of Dick Clayton's place. We rode through the night till we heard all that shooting awhile back. That's when we saw how you were riding straight into an ambush. We weren't going to sit around and watch that happen."

"I'm obliged," Halliday said, then he looked at Whelan. "That's all it was, Whelan—Latimer and Mann after my hide?"

"Latimer didn't care much about you, though. He was too keen to get after that old fool. It was Mann who said for us to wait here and gun you down. Rees don't take to you, Halliday, not one spit."

"Do you figure he's gone after Dick Clayton and his niece?"

"I guess he has. There's a heap of dollars involved. We were all gonna split it up, but I guess

Latimer and Mann would've taken the biggest share for themselves. The others were just in it for what they could get." Whelan wet his lips. "Hell, seein' as how I'm tellin' you all this, and you, too, Shelvy, you … you just gotta give me a chance."

"A chance to do what?" Shelvy asked.

Whelan gulped. "To get away. I ain't done nothin' that you should want to string me up. We ain't hit it off, but that ain't no reason to hang a man, is it?"

"I've killed for less," Shelvy told him.

Halliday could see that the man was plainly enjoying himself. But at the same time, he seemed to have become less determined to hang Whelan right away. Halliday left them and went to his horse. Getting into the saddle, he saw Shelvy drag Whelan to his feet.

Halliday rode across to them and said, "I think you'd better leave the rest to me, Tim. It's Rees Mann and me now. It seems he wants my hide, so I aim to give him the chance to get it."

"You don't want us to come along, Buck?" Shelvy asked, surprise in his voice.

"I can manage on my own."

Shelvy studied him thoughtfully for a time, before he nodded. "I guess you can at that, Buck. Has the girl got her hooks into you, maybe?"

Halliday shook his head.

"Do you think Clayton will pay if you help him?"

Halliday shrugged. "I don't know. All I know is that Mann is somewhere ahead and while he and I ride the same country, there's bound to be trouble. When we meet, I don't want anybody complicatin' the issue. Understand?"

"Whatever you say, Buck, but don't take your eyes off that sonuva. It could be that he ain't all that they claim he is, but from what I saw of him, he's damn sure of himself. He stands about like ordinary trouble is way below him. Peculiar, though, there ain't anybody who's ever seen him draw a gun. Maybe he's all bluff."

"Maybe," Halliday said dryly as he turned his sorrel away.

Shelvy grabbed Whelan and pulled him away from the rocks and pushed him toward the tree. The rest of the hands gathered in a circle and the silence which followed attracted Halliday's attention before he turned through the gateway on his way down to the flat country again. He reined-up as he heard Tim Shelvy ask;

"So, who's got somethin' against this feller? Speak up now, because this is a legal court and the condemned deserves a fair hearin'."

Whelan stood there, face gray with fear, his gaze moving across the faces of his accusers. The cowhands exchanged thoughtful looks, before Shelvy announced;

"Well, I'll start the ball rollin'. Whelan's made it clear that he don't like us, and given the chance, would be only too willin' to shoot any one of us down on sight."

"No," Whelan cried. "That ain't true. I'm through here, I told you. All I want is to—"

"Shut up, mister. You'll get your chance to say somethin' later." Shelvy looked at each of his friends. "As I was sayin', Whelan would shoot any of us down on sight, and I guess he'd best like to do it in the back. Also, he'd work for any damn jasper who gave him enough paydirt and wouldn't ask any questions. The way I see it, if he gets away from here in one piece, he'll soon link up with somebody else and cause us a heap more trouble. It just ain't in him to do an honest day's work, and I reckon a man like that should be stopped from doin' dishonest work."

Halliday noticed that some of the cowhands had trouble making up their minds. He couldn't quite understand what Shelvy had in mind, but he was aware that the cattleman was plainly

110

having the time of his life. Whelan went on sweating as Shelvy rambled on;

"We could hang him here and now, with no expense to the community a-tall. Only Lomar maybe wouldn't approve of that, especially as we ain't got anythin' proven against him, like catchin' him red-handed at rustlin', or rapin' a woman or actually murderin' someone. What we got is proof that he waited in ambush and took potshots at us. All in all, I see him as a jasper who enjoys hurtin' people. So maybe we shouldn't hang him. Maybe we should do somethin' to him which would slow him down. Make him useless to the kind of louse who's likely to hire him."

"What are you gettin' at, Tim?" a cowhand asked.

Shelvy drew his gun and pointed it at Whelan. "Get his horse," he said.

Nobody moved for a moment, but when Shelvy turned his hard-eyed stare on his men, one of them hurried off. He returned with the horse, and Whelan shifted a pace toward it and then stopped, eyeing Shelvy fearfully.

"Shoots with his right hand, don't he?" Shelvy asked, speaking to no one in particular.

Halliday heard somebody grunt in approval, then Shelvy rammed his gun against Whelan's neck.

"Put your hand on that tree, mister," he commanded.

Whelan gaped in horror.

"It's that or the rope," Shelvy hissed.

Whelan looked imploringly at the men closing in around him. One man grabbed his arm and held it to the tree. Whelan fought to push him off but two more men stepped forward and grappled with him until they had his arm held fast to the tree.

Shelvy angled his gun down slowly, taking careful aim. When the shot sounded, Whelan screamed in agony and Shelvy said, "Let him go. He ain't about to cause anyone else any grief."

Released, Whelan backed away, staring down in horror at his mangled gun hand. Then his gaze lifted to Shelvy.

"You didn't have to do that!"

"If any one of us lays eyes on you again, we'll use that rope. That I swear. Now, git!"

Whelan reached up for the pommel of the saddle with his left hand. After two unsuccessful tries, he swung into the saddle and gathered up the reins. He stared down painfully at his bleeding hand before he slipped it inside his shirt. Then he turned the horse around and glared down at Shelvy. There was so much hate in his eyes that Halliday knew this fight was far from over. But he considered that it was no longer any of his business, so he turned his sorrel out of the rocky gateway and pointed its head north. He had just cleared a clump of dry brush when Whelan reached him. The man threw a vicious, hateful look his way, spat out a curse and rode on.

It was the perfect punishment, Halliday had to admit. Then his mind turned back to Hope Clayton and her uncle. If Rees Mann had gone after them, he had a good start. He put his horse into a lope and headed for the open prairie, knowing with absolute certainty that sometime soon, he would again come face to face with Rees Mann. It was a meeting he didn't look forward to, but nothing on this earth could make him walk away from it.

While Rees Mann lived, this country wasn't big enough for them both …

SEVEN

SAME FACE, NEW SOUL

Rees Mann thought that it was time to take fresh stock of the situation in which he'd found himself.

In his first meeting with Aldo Latimer, he had carefully sized the man up to be wily, sneaky and ambitious, but was almost powerless to do anything against him. That opinion had been correct, but it no longer mattered now that Latimer was dead. Mann felt no remorse. Nor was he concerned about the fate of the others.

He halted his horse in the shade of a cottonwood clump and studied the trail ahead. He was surprised that Dick Clayton and his niece had covered so much ground in such a short time.

They were still ahead of him, although the tracks of the rig were fresh in the powdery ground along the creek bank. In two hours or perhaps three, he decided, he'd close the distance between them.

He looked at his backtrail as he had done for hours. Nobody was following him. But he knew that Halliday would certainly come. The very air about him was full of tension, as was the silence that had come down like a cloak. He wasn't unduly worried, in fact he looked forward to a showdown with the man. The drifter was going to eat his lead, and no mistake.

The issues were crystal clear to him. Clayton and his niece were ahead, Halliday was behind. The Claytons had the papers that established their rights to their property. The railroad representative was either in Parson Falls awaiting their arrival or he was already on the way to meet them. The signing over of the land would be a simple transaction, then Clayton and his niece would have their hands on the money. He could see no difficulty at all in taking it from them. He would wait for the money to be handed over, and then he'd make his move.

This, he told himself, was the very crux of the deal, so he would have to be patient. And he could think of no better way of spending that time than in the company of Dick Clayton's beautiful niece.

At first, Hope Clayton had appeared to him to be just another simple range girl. Subsequent events had shown her to be surprisingly courageous, and was one of the most spirited women he had ever met.

He came out of the shade after checking his backtrail and then he put his horse into a run and kept pushing it to maintain the pace. By mid-afternoon, he guessed from the tracks that he was no more than an hour behind his quarry. He looked at the sun and figured he'd reach them before sundown. He watered the horse at a spring, gave it a five minute rest, and then drove it hard into the hill country. Now, his gaze continually searched for the rig. Ahead, a flock of birds took to the air that told him of activity in that area. He slowed his mount and rode directly toward a steep rise.

He found a trail without any tracks, and at the top of the rise, he stopped. His gaze swept the land below him until he saw the faint outline of the rig. An attempt had been made to hide it in brush. He smiled, took out his gun and rode the horse on at a steady walk. Then he hauled rein and looked back over his trail.

There was nothing to be seen. He waited for a full minute before he called out;

"Clayton, it's me, Rees Mann. I mean you no harm, the dead opposite in fact."

There was no response.

Mann's face showed no expression as he went on;

"Latimer is dead and his outfit has disbanded. I finally realized how wrong they were. So I've come to help you as much as I can and see that you have no more trouble about transacting your business."

Mann pulled his hand back and then hurled the gun into a clearing. He then lifted his hand higher and pulled the bloodied bandanna from it.

"You can see there was trouble, Clayton. I lost one gun and many men have been killed. I'm so glad it's all behind me. Latimer told me a heap of lies, but if you think back, you'll know that at no time did I harm you or your niece. I merely carried out Latimer's orders."

Here he paused, his head cocked to hear a reply. But no sound came from the rocky country ahead of him. A frown puckered his brow. He tried again, keeping his voice flat and calm.

"If you'll remember that incident in town, I played no part in that, either. And I didn't interfere when Halliday came to your rescue. As soon as I saw how things were, I told the Latimer ranch hands to get out of town. The following morning, when Latimer told me what he had in mind, I packed my things and left. He didn't like me leavin' him so he sent his men after me. Some were killed and I was wounded, but the upshot of it is that I'm here to help you get to Parson Falls because I feel guilty about all the trouble Latimer has caused you and your niece. If you don't accept my offer, well, I'll just go on my way. I'll give you a few minutes to chew it over."

He was about to dismount when Dick Clayton's old rifle barrel pushed through the brush, and he said sharply;

"Stay put, Rees. Don't you move now."

Mann relaxed in the saddle and let the reins drop. A moment later, he heard movement down the trail and saw Hope Clayton step out from behind a boulder. She climbed a rock and made a long and careful study of the country below them. Coming back up the trail, she stopped behind Mann's horse. He removed his hat and gave her a brief nod.

"I'm alone, as you can see."

"Maybe you are, but that don't prove nothin' to me," the old man snapped. "You took Latimer's money to do his dirty work and maybe you're still takin' it. Maybe Latimer ain't dead like you say. But I don't give a hang about that one way or the other. You just tell me why we should want your help when we're only a day's ride from Parson Falls and I got the sights of my gun trained square on your guts?"

Mann shrugged easily. "There's been a lot of talk about the deal you're about to make, Clayton. I know for a fact that most of Latimer's crew would give their eyeteeth for the chance to get their hands on you and make you sign over your land to them. Now that Latimer's dead, what's to stop them from comin' after you and givin' you hell one way or another? I'd think about your niece's safety first. Some of that crowd have had their eyes on her and they haven't tried to hide it."

Clayton stepped clear of the brush, looking tired and haggard. His eyes were red-rimmed and there was a slump to his narrow shoulders. His angry stare settled on Mann and he jerked the old rifle up higher.

"I don't need your help to stop them scum from gettin' to my Hope. The first one who shows his face anywhere near her will get it shot off. As for the rest of your fancy lingo, I don't know whether to trust you of not. You got a way of provin' what you just said, mister?"

119

Mann shook his head and then showed the old man his wounded wrist. "Latimer did that."

"Who can back up what you say?"

"Nobody," Mann said.

He picked up the reins and turned the horse side-on to Clayton. Looking down at Hope, he said;

"Miss Clayton, I'm sorry I failed to convince your uncle about my intentions. But I fully understand his suspicions. If you won't let me help you, then at least take my advice. Get the hell away from here just as soon as you can. If you get caught up here, there'll be no way out for you, but down in the flat country, there's always a chance of some-body ridin' by from Parson Falls." Mann turned back to Clayton. "Will you hand me my gun?"

Clayton had already picked up the big gun. He held it thoughtfully in his left hand, weigh-ing it carefully. The weight of the gun surprised him. He then tucked his rifle under his armpit and emptied the shells into his hand. Tossing the gun back, he said. "Now you git, young feller, and stay away from us. Maybe you mean well, but, by hell, I've got this far without help from anybody and I'll go all the way into Parson Falls under my own steam, too. Now just you ride outta here and keep on goin'."

"I'll be in Parson Falls, if you need me," Mann said, then he rode past Hope, giving her another friendly nod.

He was no more than twenty yards away and looking straight down into the heat-seared distance when she walked across to her uncle.

"What if he's telling the truth, Uncle?" Hope said. "What if those other men are at this very moment closing in on us?"

"Then a few of 'em are gonna get buckshot where they won't like it, girl. Now go see how the horse is doin'."

"I've already checked on him, Uncle," Hope told him, looking disturbed. "He's exhausted and can't go another step till morning."

"It's got to. We can't camp out here, not with Mann knowin' our whereabouts. Hell, it didn't take him long to find our rig, did it? You reckon that don't prove how sneaky he is? I tell you, he's out to help nobody but himself, that one."

"He's hurt, Uncle," Hope said as she watched the tall, straight-backed gun hand ride away.

Clayton snorted. "Sure he's hurt. I'm hurt, a lot of other folks are hurt. He reckons Latimer shot him in the wrist. Well, from what I know of Aldo Latimer, he hasn't the guts to tackle somebody like Rees Mann. I'm sayin' it now, loud and clear—he's lyin'. I don't know what he's up to, ridin' in here and pretendin' to offer us help. Maybe he figured on gettin' us off our guard so he could jump me."

Clayton fingered his unruly hair back and checked his rifle again. He then stormed back into the brush and made his way down to where the unharnessed horse stood, head down, almost out on its feet. He made a thorough study of its coat and condition. Then cursing under his breath, he returned to find his niece building a fire. He let out a deep sigh. "Might as well light it, girl, and to hell with the smoke. Mann knows where we are and maybe some others do, too. We'll give them an open invitation … but we won't be here for the party."

"What do you have in mind, Uncle?" Hope asked, seeing a gleam of cunning in the old-timer's eyes.

"I got it in mind to drag the rig away, girl. It won't be so damned hard going downhill. "Won't have to go far, neither. Then we'll put the horse in the shafts and let him rest the night. Come morning, I'll drive him all the way to Parson Falls, even if it kills the both of us."

Hope lifted her head and worked cramp from her neck and shoulders. The sun had burned her all that day and what she wanted most just then was a bath and then a long, uninterrupted sleep. She got the fire going and put on the coffeepot. Then, while her uncle checked the area for the best route to drag the rig, she made up their evening meal.

Zac Whelan packed salt on his butchered hand and wrapped a strip of old blanket around it. He then mounted his horse, let it drink from the creek while he fought to stop from crying out against the pain. If he had a gun, he doubted if he could use it.

Sweat ran in rivers down his face. Despite his pain and recurring waves of panic, his mind clung to the thought that Rees Mann was somewhere up ahead. He had to find him and tell him what had happened. Mann had ridden out before the fight was over, and Whelan hated him for that. But he admitted that the gunman had at least showed some sense. But he still felt that Mann should have stood his ground a little longer.

Suddenly, he felt terribly alone. He kept looking about him, imagining that at any moment, somebody—Buck Halliday most likely—would jump up out of the ground and finish him off. He had to stay alive, because one of these days he would get his revenge on Tim Shelvy. He'd watch the man suffer just like Shelvy had watched him.

The sun went down behind the western rim, and with the dusk came the cool air. He left the creek and followed the ruts left by the Clayton rig. The jolting of the horse under him caused him discomfort for the next hour, then darkness began to swallow up the range and he looked about for a place to make camp. He had just selected a flat piece of country surrounded by rocks and brush on three sides when he saw Rees Mann.

Mann was astride his horse under the shadows of a tall cottonwood. He had his gun in his holster and his hands were locked together on his saddle pommel. He looked completely relaxed as he studied Whelan, who drew rein, smothered a cry of pain, and said;

"Am I glad I caught up with you!"

Mann's gaze shifted over the big man's frame, taking in the empty holster, the bandaged hand, the brush-torn clothes and the pain-riddled face.

"I'm surprised to see you up here," he said.

Whelan shuddered. "That Shelvy bunch fixed us up real good. Latimer's dead, so there's only you and me now."

"What about Halliday?" Mann asked as Whelan rode up.

"He cut out on his own. I reckon I'm in front of him, but not by much."

Whelan pulled his bandage off and showed Mann his ruined hand. After Mann studied it blandly, Whelan said;

"Shelvy did that to me. Hell, you've gotta help me get square with that bastard. I'll get another gun and I'll learn how to use it in my left hand. I know others who have done it."

"I've heard that, too."

Whelan's eyes lit up. "Maybe one day some medic will be able to fix me up like new. We can still be a team. I'll do anythin' you say. Right now we can catch up with that old buzzard, get his deeds and still sell his place."

Mann nodded calmly. Taking the man's silence as a vague acceptance, Whelan brightened and said;

"We'll make it. Could be we might even take the girl along with us, eh?"

"Now there's a thought," Mann said, then he turned his horse and looked back along the long trail he'd taken a half-hour ago. "You ready to ride?"

"Where?"

"Up there where Clayton and his niece have made camp. I checked on them earlier, but

Clayton got the drop on me. I decided not to take any fool chances and to wait till morning before I approached them again. But now, waitin' seems the wrong thing to do, what with you along to keep the girl busy while I take the old man out."

Whelan licked nervously at his lips and hugged his hand to his chest. "I ain't exactly up to handlin' that hellcat. Maybe, like you said, we should wait till mornin'."

"Time's runnin' out. If Clayton gets away tonight, he might make it all the way to Parson Falls. They got a fire goin' but I figure it's just to fool me. That old coot wouldn't be that stupid to show the world where they are. We'll ride in slow. When you sight the girl, make sure she doesn't give us any trouble. Let's go."

Whelan wiped his face on his sleeve and was reminded again of the beating Halliday had given him. He knew he couldn't achieve much on his own, but with Mann along, who knew …?

That settled in his mind, he followed Mann up the trail, his gaze continually searching for the first sign of life. Every nerve end seemed alive. Finally, they reached the fire which had all but burned down, when Whelan said;

"Looks like you're right. Hell, workin' with you is gonna be a breeze compared to workin' with

126

Aldo Latimer. That fat shoat didn't know how to think things through. He made a heap of mistakes, and some I even warned him about. Only thing was, I didn't know how you'd feel about anybody doin' that."

"Work your way up through the timber," Mann told him. "You can see the tracks. Their horse would have to be spent, the way he's been pushin' it. If that's so … we'll have them."

Whelan made a careful inspection of the tracks and smiled in satisfaction. "Seems to me you could be right. That old codger got off here and was likely pulling it up the slope. Must be that his horse is out on its feet." He looked about him and suddenly he remembered he was defenseless. "Clayton's got that old rifle and the girl ain't no slouch when it comes to usin' a whip. I reckon we'd best be right careful from here on in. No tellin' what they got planned for anybody tryin' to jump 'em."

"So go and see," Mann said. "Clayton will hole-up where he can get the most protection. And just remember … where Clayton is, you'll find his niece."

Whelan frowned heavily as he looked ahead. The silence unsettled him. There was only enough moonlight to throw distorted shadows over the landscape.

He walked his horse down the narrow trail, taking half an hour to reach the end of the long slope. He was about to ride into the moonlight when he saw a cluster of boulders just ahead and brush behind them thick enough to conceal a horse and rig.

He dismounted, finger-tipped sweat from his top lip and drew down a ragged breath. His nervousness was increasing by the minute and at each slight sound of wind-stirred brush, he gave a start. But the worst part for him was the absence of Rees Mann. He hadn't sighted Mann for the last ten minutes.

He didn't have a gun and had no clear idea of what might be in front of him. He was still trying to make a decision when a blast of gunfire broke the night's stillness. He let out a sharp cry and bolted for the cover of the rocks. In so doing, he almost ran into a second rifle blast. He veered to the left, running as fast as his fat legs would carry him. On the way, he saw Hope crouched high on a rocky slope, moonlight gleaming off her long hair. He charged into the brush, tripped on a deadfall and fell. As soon as he hit the ground, he scrambled back to his feet. His hand hurt like crazy and having to hold it against his chest made his running awkward. But he trudged on, fear tugging at his senses.

It was only when he reached a point beyond the boulders and the brush and was about a hundred feet from where the young woman crouched, that he saw Rees Mann again.

To his relief, Mann was riding hard now, galloping his horse past the boulders.

Whelan stopped and drew down a deep breath. He was about to shout when he saw that Mann was coming straight at him. He leaned against a tree and decided to leave it all to him.

Mann could kill Clayton easily now and then there'd be only the girl.

Mann crossed a moonlit stretch and Whelan lifted his hand in greeting. Mann had his gun out. His gaze settled on Whelan and a thin smile twisted at the corners of his mouth.

Whelan frowned, not understanding what Mann had to grin about. Then Mann's gun leveled on him. As a cry of disbelief rose to Whelan's lips, Mann's bullet slammed into his chest. Whelan's body was nailed to the tree by the impact, and then a second bullet blew his chest open.

EIGHT

AN ENEMY
TURNED FRIEND

The only sound to be heard was the tramp of
Dick Clayton's boots on the hard ground.

Rees Mann saw him leave the cluster of rocks,
step forward hesitantly, then hobble along the
narrow trail and stop. The rifle in the old man's
hands jerked up and settled threateningly on his
chest. Mann took little notice of it, turning his
gaze to where Hope Clayton was standing, her
face deep in thought. When Hope came up to
her uncle's side, Mann said;

"I heard the shots and knew Whelan was making trouble for you. I'd seen him from the ridge
half an hour before, but I was too far from you
to give you warnin' and not close enough to him

to stop him. Regardless of your refusal of my earlier offer, I just couldn't let him ride through here. He was acting like a loon, the way he came tearing across the flats, hair flowing in the wind, clothes torn and bloodied and—"

"You saw all that," the old man put in. "How?"

"It wasn't all that dark," Mann responded calmly, then he drew his horse closer and patted its neck, a thin smile running along his lips.

Hope regarded him intently, as though seeing him for the first time. Her previous opinion of him had led her to expect only brutality from him, even murder. But since he had saved her from Whelan, she thought she might have to change her opinion, even if her uncle still didn't trust the man.

"Are you all right, Mr. Mann?" Hope asked.

"I'm fine, Miss Clayton. I'll stay only to bury this poor fool and then I'll be on my way again. But be careful. If Whelan made it this far, maybe some of the others can make it, too. You could be in for more trouble tonight and I wouldn't stay too long out in the open."

"No need to bury that skunk," the old man said. "Buzzards look after their own."

Hope looked quickly at her uncle when Mann let out a chuckle.

"You've got a lot of hate in you, old man, but I guess I don't blame you. In this kind of country and with the business you have to negotiate, it doesn't pay to be over-friendly with anybody. I'm glad I was able to help you and your niece and perhaps when you're finished with your business and have no longer any need to be suspicious of me, we can meet up again."

Mann's look went to Hope, causing her to blush. She saw him as a man who took pride in his appearance. He sat his horse gracefully and looked for all the world like he'd just dressed after a good night's rest. His clothes, despite the country he'd traveled, still looked neat, and his face was that of a man who had nothing to fear. Then Hope said;

"You don't have to go, Mr. Mann. I have a medicine kit in the rig. Let me look at your wrist. It's the least we can do for you."

The old man swung on her and growled; "Now see here, girl, who the hell runs this—?"

"Uncle Dick, stop being such a bellower. After what's happened, even you have to admit that Mr. Mann is on our side. Why else would he kill that man? Doesn't that prove to you that all the bad might be behind him? It follows then that everything he's said to us could have a ring of truth to it."

Mann watched the old-timer wrestle with his conscience. He realized that the business this pair still had to transact could be difficult. But he had won the girl's confidence, and that was an important victory. He shifted about in the saddle, and said;

"My wrist could use some attention, Miss Clayton, but only if your uncle agrees to you attending to it. At the worst it'll give me some pain on the way to Parson Falls, but I doubt if I'll die from it."

"I want to repay you at least a little for what you've done, Mr. Mann," Hope said, and walked past her uncle, ignoring him.

The oldster studied Mann gravely as the gunfighter came down off his horse. The moment Mann's boots touched the ground, Clayton jerked his rifle up and snapped;

"Okay, she can tend to your wrist! Meantime, I want you to hand over your gun."

"And if somebody comes ridin' in here?"

"Then I'll likely give it back to you. I'm too close to my destination now to start trustin' anybody."

Mann unbuckled his gunbelt and handed it over. Dropping the belt across a bony shoulder, Clayton stepped aside to let Mann past, then he fell in behind him and followed him to the rocks.

Hope had opened a small medicine box and had already spread out ointment, iodine and bandages. Mann took his canteen from his pommel and poured water over the wound. Hope then made a brief inspection.

"It doesn't appear to be too bad. How did it happen?"

"Latimer," he said, as he let Hope bandage the wrist. When she had finished, he worked his hand a few times and then nodded in gratitude before he walked to where their horse was standing in the shadows of the boulders. After an inspection of the horse, he said to Clayton;

"If you like, I'll exchange my horse for yours. He might not be trained to pull a rig, but he'll come to accept it after awhile. You and your niece can then go on while I wait behind and keep watch on your trail."

The old man frowned heavily at him, and asked;

"You'd do that for us?"

"Why not? Time is runnin' out for us all. The sooner you get to Parson Falls, the sooner you can tie up your business and the sooner I can relax in your niece's company again."

Hope came across to her uncle's side. "Why not, Uncle Dick? It's such a generous offer! And it's one we can't refuse."

Her uncle shook his head uncertainly. "I don't know, girl. I've never been able to trust anybody in the past."

"But we'd be in Parson Falls and Mr. Mann'd be out here, wouldn't he?" Hope pleaded.

The old man walked across to Mann's horse, studied it for a time, and said;

"We'll do it. And I'm grateful. Hell, mebbe I've had you wrong all this time. Maybe you could have changed."

But Clayton kept Mann's gunbelt over his shoulder as he disappeared into the brush. A short time later, he emerged, pulling the rig. He tossed the gunbelt into the back and now he threw out a suspicious glance as Mann came to help him. But Rees Mann ignored him, got the fresh horse into the shafts, and after calming it, worked the reins over its head and linked them on the driving seat. He then crossed to Clayton's weary horse.

All this time, Hope had kept a close eye on him, watching his effortless movements, impressed by his fine clothes. She thought of the place she and her uncle had left. It wasn't big, but if worked properly, it could support a family.

A flush rose to her cheeks when she realized she was including Rees Mann in her thoughts.

And why not, she asked herself? He'd been the only person to help her, except for Halliday, of course.

Buck Halliday.

Hope realized with a shock that she hadn't even thought of him during the previous twenty-four hours. They had left him behind, had sneaked away and made him fend for himself, tricked him into protecting them from Aldo Latimer.

So what had become of him?

Then her uncle called and helped her into the rig. The old man got up beside her, then reached back and picked up Rees Mann's gunbelt. He weighed it in his hand thoughtfully for a time before he tossed it down and said;

"I hope you won't be needin' it. I hope that bunch has learned its lesson. Leave Whelan's carcass where they can see it, and maybe they'll know exactly what they're up against. Later, when my horse is ready to be ridden, get him to Parson Falls. You'll be welcome as all get-out to join us in a celebration."

136

Mann looked Hope's way and smiled. "I'll look forward to it."

Then he stepped away and buckled his gun-belt about his waist.

When Clayton drove the rig away from the clearing and past Zac Whelan's body, Mann stood with his legs planted wide and waved. Hope returned the gesture just before she went from sight around a line of boulders.

Mann stoked up the fire and added more wood. Soon flames leaped into the moonlit sky. He unrolled his gear, spreading it out on the ground by the fire. Then he went into the shadows of the boulders and settled down to wait. From what Whelan had told him, he had only one worry … Buck Halliday. The big drifter would come after him, he was sure. Mann knew Halliday was a lot like himself, unable to refuse the challenge of a man who was near his equal with a gun. Mann checked his .45 and turned his bandaged right wrist this way and that. Hope Clayton had done a good job, and he found that as soon as he worked circulation into it, he could draw his gun with all his former speed.

NINE

THE ULTIMATUM

Buck Halliday heard the gunshots and drew rein. Then he peered down into the moonlit country but nothing stirred. As soon as the echo of the gunshots faded, there was no sound above the soft wash of the cool night wind through the brush.

He waited ten minutes before he went on.

He knew that Zac Whelan was ahead of him, and so was Rees Mann. One of them must have fired off those shots, and either of them, given the chance, would gun him down. So he kept to the shadows until he saw where the tracks of a rig had disappeared at the edge of a stretch of hard ground.

He came out of the saddle, hitched the horse and carefully checked the ground, moving in an ever-widening circle until he picked up the tracks again. He was standing there, contemplating his next move when a single gunshot disturbed the peace about him.

Halliday went straight to the ground, his gun already in his hand. But the shot was not followed by a second, and the bullet hadn't come his way. He waited a full minute before he risked moving again. As far as he could make out, the shot had come from behind a set of boulders a hundred yards ahead of him.

Getting to his feet, he headed for them. He made a wide circle and came up behind the rocks to find a shabby-coated horse lying on its side, with a bullet hole in its head.

A close inspection told Halliday that it was Dick Clayton's animal. He was trying to work out what had happened when he saw the body of Zac Whelan in a pool of moonlight. Whelan was on his stomach and the ground around him was covered with blood.

Halliday went to the body and turned it over with his boot. He saw the two bullet holes and then his gaze took in the empty holster.

Whelan's killer had gunned down an unarmed man.

Dick Clayton? Yes, he could do it. The man was a wily old fox, so concerned about getting the money for his ranch that Halliday couldn't put it past him to shoot before asking questions.

Yet the fact that Whelan had come this way, trailing Mann as well as the Claytons, indicated that Whelan had plenty on his mind. Whatever it was, the fat gun hand had failed.

Halliday turned away from the body and was making his way toward his horse when a rider burst from cover below him. His gun jerked up and he threw himself to the side. Bullets ripped into the ground where his shoulder made contact and he felt a sharp tug of pain along his neck. He rolled, hearing the thunder of hoof beats coming closer. He finally stopped rolling in the cover of dry brush and saw Rees Mann boring down on him.

Mann was grinning evilly. Halliday pushed himself to his knees and braced himself. But at the last moment, Mann swung his mount away, and as he did so, Halliday saw that Mann was riding the sorrel.

Anger worked through him and he jumped to his feet and emptied his gun at Mann's back.

The bullets ricocheted off rock and then the gunfighter was out of range.

Halliday refilled his gun and stood there cursing. His mind worked feverishly now, trying to make some sense of this whole affair. Whelan was dead, but to have come this far, he had to have been on horseback. Clayton and the girl were still missing, so too the rig. Now Mann was highballing toward Parson Falls on his horse.

Which left him out here alone.

He knew with certainty that he would have to find a horse quickly or Mann would succeed in making him look a total ass.

Halliday listened to the fading drum of hoof beats and began to walk. But two hours of following the sorrel's tracks left him with no greater reward than weariness.

He looked out over the night-shrouded plain, the moonlight dim but he could see the rig's tracks and near them the tracks of his sorrel.

Tightening his gunbelt, he went down the slope and moved in a steady walking pace. He wasn't sure how far it was to Parson Falls but was determined to reach town and pick up Mann's trail there. It wasn't just the matter of a stolen horse, he told himself—it was something much bigger. So big, in fact, that it wouldn't end until he faced Rees Mann down.

It was hate—deep, unrelenting, eternal …

The edge of Buck Halliday's tongue rasped across his dry, cracked lips. His throat burned and his feet ached. But he walked on, looking ahead, hoping for the sight of a building that would mean water, rest and another horse.

The silence crowded in on him as the sun rose. Impatience stung him. Aches had already risen and died in his legs and arms but he walked on, numbed like a zombie, his mind a turmoil of bitter thoughts.

Yet behind the screen of confusion, he found himself looking at the image of Hope Clayton that formed in his mind.

Dick Clayton had left him to fight a war that was not his. He had no idea of Hope's involvement in the trickery. He reminded himself that at the outset of this trip, his anger had been directed at her as much as it had been at her uncle. Why this was so, he couldn't remember now. He saw her only as she had been in that pass, the moonlight shining on her hair, her face so angelic and full of need—yet frightened.

Was she who she pretended to be, a woman who had known no man before?

Halliday didn't know. He walked on, taking the image of her with him, feeling emotions stirring deep inside that kept him struggling on. One day he would find out, he promised himself.

The sun was up now and the day's heat was beginning to close in around him. The sand under his feet would soon be so hot it would burn through his soles and scorch his feet.

How far now to Parson Falls …?

Mile after mile he trudged on, kicking up sand, feeling the steady increase of heat from the sky-climbing sun. A cluster of clouds sat on the horizon in the far eastern portion of the sky. All about him was the desert, a wasteland of loneliness, heat and thirst.

He stopped suddenly, lifting a hand to shade his eyes. For a time he dared not believe that there was a shape in front of him. He knew the tricks that thirst and heat could play on a man's mind. But as he stared, the shape took on depth and substance. A hill. And beyond it the outline of timber—deep green treetops against a brilliant blue sky.

He pushed himself on, but he could barely drag one foot after the other, making such slow progress that the hill didn't seem to be getting any closer. He kept on, his eyes fixed on the hill, the gunbelt on his waist burning his skin through his pants until he thought about discarding it. But he knew that would be foolish. A horse and a gun, these were the vital necessities in the West. He had lost his horse, he couldn't afford to lose his gun.

Hours passed.

Suddenly, the hill loomed before him, its rocks standing heat-seared in the broiling sun. The trees turned out to be cottonwoods. Good. Where there were cottonwoods, there was water. Plenty of water.

A rise of panic struck him. What if the water had been consumed by the drought? He didn't think he could go on much further without water, certainly not into the blast of another desert sun. He swung his arms, and although they ached considerably, he kept pushing himself, refusing to give in. It would be either death or salvation—there was no in-between.

He entered the shade of the cottonwoods and stopped. The relief he felt was so great that he felt like dropping to his knees and digging his hands into the earth. He discarded this crazy thought and continued into the trees. But the grass was dry, brown, without moisture, almost like straw. A feeling of hopelessness began to take hold of him.

Then he heard the thunder of hoof beats.

He swung about, an exultant cry forming on his lips. A horse meant getting out of here.

Then Rees Mann came thundering from behind a boulder, his gun blasting. A bullet tugged at Halliday's sleeve before he shook off his confusion and realized what was happening.

He dropped to the ground, his gun coming quickly to hand. He fired off three quick shots as Mann rode past, the horse's hoofs missing his head by a whisker and no more.

Halliday rolled to his feet, looked anxiously about him and then broke into a staggering run. More shots ripped at him. He felt the burn of a bullet along his shoulder and another at his wrist. He didn't give a damn—he cared only for survival.

He threw himself headlong into a clump of dry brush and a branch tore open his right cheek. Blood flowed into his mouth and he swallowed, fighting to remain conscious, knowing that to give in now was to present himself with a ticket to Boothill.

He forced himself onto his elbows. The pounding of hoofs had now stopped. He lifted his head and his gaze swept the heat-seared clearing.

There was no sign of Rees Mann.

He waited a few minutes more. His clothes tore on the dry brush, throwing out enough noise to attract another blast of gunfire that sent bullets whining around his head.

Cursing, he crawled deeper into the brush. He had just stopped in a hollow, when Mann called;

"Halliday, hear me good. I'm going on to Parson Falls. Twice I've tried to kill you and twice I've failed. If you try to follow me … I won't fail a third time."

"You have my horse, mister, so how do you expect me to travel?" Halliday called back, his voice no more than a croak.

"On hands and knees, if you have to. Just don't come after me."

Halliday rose to his haunches. Even though he could see clear down into the lower section of this oasis, he could see no sign of Rees Mann.

Then the hoof beats started up again. His horse broke into a canter and finally a gallop. He stood watching Rees Mann and the sorrel fade into the distance.

TEN

TIME DOESN'T COUNT

Dick Clayton impatiently paced the rooming house dining room floor. Each time he reached the window, he peered intently across to the closed doors of the bank.

A short time after reaching Parson Falls, he had gone straight to the railroad company offices located midtown. There he'd met Camer Wilkinson, who had immediately wired company headquarters. A wire had come back within the hour telling Wilkinson to sign and witness all the necessary paperwork.

In the oldster's hand now, he had the railroad company's check for ten thousand dollars and was waiting for Hope to come down for breakfast.

When the bank opened, he'd cash the check and leave town, heading for a place where he wasn't known. Only then would he be able to relax.

Rees Mann found him with little trouble. Mann walked in, dusting his range hat down his brush-torn clothes. His gaze traveled the room before they settled on Clayton. He strode over to him and said;

"Everything finalized?"

The old man nodded and patted his shirt pocket. "All I've got to do now is wait for the bank to open its doors. Then I can get our money and get to hell out of here. I'm grateful to you for what you did for us. I've been thinkin' about it all and I realize now that without your help we wouldn't have stood a chance. When you lent me your horse, that just about sealed things for us. I've got him out back, still in the rig and I'll pay you double his worth, if you want to sell him."

"Fair enough," Mann said. He looked at his pocket watch. It was five minutes to ten. "Might as well see it through all the way," he said. "I'll stay with you until you finish your business with the bank. Then maybe we'll have a drink and share a meal before you leave. Meantime, while we're headin' for the bank, I'd like you to think about my comin' further with you. I'm mighty attracted to your niece and I have reason to believe she feels the same way about me. I'm through with gunfighting. I've learned there are other ways of making a livin', ways that are far more rewarding."

Clayton looked surprised. "You sure you want that? Hell, I always figured that your kind never changed."

Mann smiled shyly as he fitted his hat to his head. "My kind don't often meet up with a woman like your niece, Mr. Clayton. She deserves a lot better than working on that small ranch of yours. I've got money put aside and I want to buy my own place, have others working for me. If you want, maybe we could come to some arrangement on a business deal. I'll always have my guns to protect us, no matter if I'm not hirin' them out anymore."

Clayton licked his lips, an eager light showing in his eyes. "That doesn't sound too unattractive. Let me think about it, eh? I been worried about all this money anyway, and I don't reckon I can last forever. Besides, Hope will have to get herself settled down sooner or later. Maybe, just maybe …"

His voice trailed off and he stood there nodding his head. Suddenly, he drew himself tall and said;

"All right, come on then. The sooner we get this business done, the sooner I'm gonna get a drink into me. Hell, crossin' that desert sure took a lot outta me."

Mann let the old man lead the way across the street to the bank. Clayton went in past the clerk who had just opened the doors and stopped at the grille behind which a second clerk waited.

The clerk took Clayton's check, smiled and said;

"We were told that you might be coming, Mr. Clayton. It will be no trouble to pack the money into a case for you, but I strongly advise, what with the ruffians who are in town at the moment, that you take some spending money and leave the rest for us to transfer to a bank of your choice."

"I'll take the cash," Clayton told him. "And don't you fret none about anybody takin' it from me. This here's Rees Mann … my partner."

The clerk looked Mann over coolly, clearly not impressed. Mann held the fellow's stare evenly for a moment, then walked to the door. He waited there, scrubbing a hand down the back of his neck. When he saw Clayton coming out, he stepped onto the boardwalk. Two men were standing outside the rooming house foyer, a couple of yards apart. There was a sprinkling of people at the other end of the street but not many people were in this section of town. Then Hope appeared in the rooming house doorway, looking fresh and dainty in a brand new dress. She smiled broadly when she saw her uncle come jauntily across to her.

But Clayton was only halfway across the street when the two men went for their guns. Clayton froze, then threw an anxious look Mann's way. Hope spun, saw the two men and let out a scream.

The scream was drowned in a sudden eruption of gunfire.

Hope saw her uncle go down, the case in his hand dropping from his grasp. He hit the ground and threw a hand over the case as more bullets thudded into his body. By then, Mann had brought out his gun and was punching off shots. The two gun hands had stepped to the edge of the boardwalk, close to Mann. His vicious gunfire cut them down. Hope screamed again as both men staggered back under the impact of lead. Then a deathlike silence settled on the street, and Hope dropped her hands from her face.

Rees Mann was standing in the street, his gun still smoking. On his face was a look of profound satisfaction that chilled her to the bone. Then

Mann went to her uncle's side and turned him over. When Hope reached them, Mann looked up and shook his head.

Within the space of seconds, a large crowd had gathered. Among them was the local sheriff, who quickly took charge. Mann drew him aside and spoke quietly to him for some time before the lawman inspected the dead men and announced;

"Had my eye on them the past couple days. Had the look of desperados about them, and I guess I was right." He turned to Hope, "Miss Clayton, the whole town's real sorry about this. But there was nothing we could do and I guess you were lucky that man was along. We'll take your uncle to the undertaker's. Meantime, you'd best go back to your room and rest."

Mann reached down and plucked the case from the ground. He took the shocked Hope Clayton's arm and led her away. In the foyer, he told the clerk to lock the case in the safe and to guard it with his life. He then escorted Hope up the stairs.

As soon as Hope saw the bed, she threw herself down and sobbed uncontrollably into the pillow. Mann waited until she had cried herself into a quieter frame of mind, before he said;

"Don't worry about a thing. I'll see to all the arrangements. Wait here for me and don't let anybody in."

Hope didn't answer him. Mann closed the door quietly and locked it, then he dropped the key into his pocket and went down to the foyer, the room crowded with curious townsfolk. He eyed the people warily for a time before he said;

"Get out of here and get on with your business. Those two tried to rob an old man and failed. So get out of here or you'll answer to me!"

Mann walked out of the rooming house and up the boardwalk to the law office where the sheriff was leaning against the overhang, his hat pushed to the back of his head, his stare fixed solemnly. As Mann arrived, he turned and went back inside, and when Mann entered the law office, he closed the door. Walking to his desk, the lawman stood behind it and said; "Plenty of townsmen have heard about you, Mr. Mann."

"That doesn't surprise me, Sheriff," Mann told him easily. "In fact, I'm surprised you don't seem to know me."

"I'm new in the job. Two months, in fact. Before that I was in Colorado. Couldn't get my kind of work in these parts, then this job came up."

"You look the kind who'll make a good fist of it," Mann said, hooking his thumbs in his gun-belt. "Now, what did you want to see me about?"

"There was a heap of money involved," the law-man said.

"Ten thousand dollars," Mann admitted, and smiled thinly. "But don't fret about it. It belongs to the girl now. As soon as she's fit to travel, I'll get her rig ready and help her out of here."

"Where?"

"Where she can forget, Sheriff. Her uncle was the only kin she had left in the world."

"What about you?"

Mann smiled again and ran a hand through his hair. His gaze remained fixed on the lawman. "I was taken on as a partner, Sheriff. You can check with the bank, if you like. As I remember, Clayton mentioned the partnership to one of the bank clerks."

"I've already checked," the lawman said.

"Then the rest of it is simple," Mann said casually. "You bury Clayton and I take the girl where she wants to go. The dead men don't worry you, do they?"

The lawman pursed his lips and shrugged. "I guess only the living should worry a man in my position. But then, as you said, everything you said to me tallies up. However, I want you out of my town as soon as possible, as much for the girl's sake as mine."

Mann smiled again. "I think I know what you mean, Sheriff. I'll go, and it'll save us both a lot of worryin'."

Mann walked out of the jailhouse into a town that shimmered under an intense heat. Calmly, he looked toward the hills. Somewhere in that blaze of desert, Buck Halliday was coming after him. Mann thought about that and worked out a plan for himself.

That done, he retired to the saloon and sat, hardly moving, at a table in the corner. He had downed four whiskies before he felt the tension leave his body. Then, stepping out onto the boardwalk, he crossed to the rooming house and took the stairs to Hope's room.

He let himself in and sat talking to her for some time, telling her of the places where she could find happiness.

Hope didn't know what to say to him. Even though she couldn't deny that she felt obligated to him, she couldn't forget the look on his face when he had cut down those two men. The enjoyment she'd seen there still sent a chill up her spine.

Had he really changed? Or was this a pretence that she couldn't see through?

She didn't know the answer to that.

"Where would you suggest that we go?"

"There's good land on offer in California. Most people are after gold there, but not us. No, sir. Gold is too risky. You see, Hope, those towns will need meat. The men and women who forget the gold and start the ranches now will be the ones who in the end will strike it rich."

Hope wiped her tear-stained face. "What about Uncle Dick?"

"The sheriff said he'll take care of the arrangements. I'll have the rig ready and waiting straight after the ceremony. With your money and what I have stashed away, we'll be able to buy the best ranch available and fill it with stock."

"You and me?"

Mann went to her. "Why not? I had your uncle's trust before he died. And don't forget I killed those men for him and for you. But that part of my life is over now. There can be no more killings for me, no more Latimers and no more Whelans. I just want to buy a place of our own and work it, sweat like hell and get plenty of blisters for my trouble."

He looked longingly at her, letting his gaze sweep over her body.

"And I want a woman, Hope, a woman to share it with me."

Hope shook her head and walked to the window. She pulled the curtains back and then she gasped;

"Buck!"

Mann froze for a brief instant and then he stepped across the room and pushed her away from the window. Hope let out a cry as his grip bruised her arm. She stood back and saw deep hatred take hold of him. At that moment, she knew that all her fears had been well founded.

Mann swung about, brushing her aside on his way to the door.

"What is it?" Hope called out. "What are you going to do?"

"Stay put! And don't come anywhere near the street."

Hope felt a deep chill course through her body. Then the door slammed and she rushed at it as the key turned in the lock.

Halliday was in danger! Desperately, she hammered her fists against the oaken door, but in vain.

Exhausted, she went back to the window and lifted it.

Riding a mule in the company of a bewhiskered old-timer, Halliday had stopped in the middle of the street. It seemed to Hope that he was thanking the old man. There was a brief waving of arms before the old man accepted some money. Desperately now, she leaned out the window and called;

"Buck! Rees Mann's on his way down the stairs. I think he plans to kill you!"

Halliday looked up at her. But almost at the same time, he saw Mann striding across the boardwalk. There was a good-sized crowd in the street but Mann charged through, sending several people staggering out of his way. He stepped into the street and Halliday stood looking at him, legs spread. A long silence fell between them, that Mann finally broke.

"Damn you, Halliday!"

"It's you who's damned," Halliday said, then Mann's hand flashed down to his side.

His draw was so fast it brought a gasp from some of the people watching. His gun came level as Hope Clayton screamed. Then she covered her face with her hands.

In the street, Buck Halliday stood his ground. No expression showed on his face, not even when the bullet slammed into his shoulder. His draw was a trifle slower than Mann's, but his aim was more accurate. His bullet tore Mann's neck open. Mann went down on his knees and knelt there in the street, wildly shaking his head, sending blood spraying into the dust.

Then Mann made a gurgling sound and fell onto his face.

For three days, Buck Halliday recovered in a bed in back of the medic's house, impatient to get back on his feet, knowing that to try it would be foolish. He was sorry to hear of the old man's demise and was worried about it for Hope's sake. Then on the fourth afternoon, the old medic released him.

He went to the saloon and quenched his thirst for half an hour. Then he went up to Hope Clayton's room. He found her sitting on the edge of her bed, hands clasped on her lap, looking sadly up at him.

He went to her and she rose, shook her head for a moment, then threw herself into his arms. Halliday held her as she cried, stroking her hair as she clung to him, all the time delighting in the freshness of her skin.

Nothing in this world would drag him from her room tonight.

Hope sat him on the bed and took off his boots. She stood there looking down at him,